Dealing with the Dead

———

ALSO BY ALAIN MABANCKOU

African Psycho
Broken Glass
Memoirs of a Porcupine
Black Bazaar
Tomorrow I'll Be Twenty
The Lights of Pointe-Noire
Black Moses
The Death of Comrade President

Dealing with the Dead

Alain Mabanckou

—

First published in Great Britain in 2025 by
SERPENT'S TAIL
an imprint of Profile Books Ltd
29 Cloth Fair
London EC1A 7JQ
www.serpentstail.com

Originally published in French as *Le Commerce des Allongés* © Editions du Seuil, 2022

1 3 5 7 9 10 8 6 4 2

Typeset in Tramuntana Text by MacGuru Ltd
Designed by Nicky Barneby @ Barneby Ltd

Printed and bound in Great Britain by
CPI Group (UK) Ltd, Croydon CR0 4YY

A CIP catalogue record for this book is available from the British Library.

ISBN 978 1 80081 770 8
eISBN 978 1 80081 772 2

to my mother, Pauline Kengué,
whose stories appear here, more or less

to my father, Roger Kimangou,
who liked to contradict my mother's version

to the young people of Goma, and Bukavu (DRC),
for their warm welcome
while I finished this book

Dealing with the Dead

Alain Mabanckou

——

THE LONGEST DREAM
OF YOUR DEATH

———

New Life

—

YOU TELL YOURSELF OVER AND OVER till you come to believe it: your new life started an hour ago, when a shock ripped through the earth around you, and you felt yourself being sucked up by a cyclone, then flung down where you're lying right now, on a heap of earth topped with a brand-new wooden cross.

'I breathe! I live!' you murmured to yourself in triumph.

But now, with daylight peeking over the horizon, you're not so sure. You're haunted by images of your last few hours, a dead man trapped in a coffin, borne in great pomp to his final resting place, here in the cemetery of Frère-Lachaise.

Try as you may, you can't stop dwelling on the memory of the long procession escorting you through the main streets of Pointe-Noire. The parading of a corpse before burial is common practice in this town; people embrace it as a mark of homage to the deceased, giving them a lively send-off. You are carried by six square-shouldered colossi with rippling muscles, wearing white suits and shiny black shoes with pointed tips. Their job is to execute orders, not to wonder how the person they're carrying came to die. They'll stick to the route prescribed by the bereaved families, throughout the long procession their voices will stay silent.

Sealed up in the coffin, trailed along endless winding streets, you consider what will happen at your journey's end. You've seen funeral processions pass through the rue du Joli-Soir where you lived with your grandmother till the time of your death. So you know you'll end up at Frère-Lachaise, and that there you'll be just one among thousands upon thousands of dead. If you're lucky you'll get a few visitors a year besides your grandmother, Mâ Lembé. You'll find sweet bunches of flowers laid on your gravestone on All Saints' or Independence Day, though somewhat ironically in the latter case, since your death is linked to this day of national celebration. Once you've been laid in the earth, time will start to do its work, and for all their good intentions, the people who knew you will gradually forget, till one dry season comes when not a soul ventures forth to your tomb. Weeds will stifle it, lizards will haunt it, and black snakes too – those 'souls of no fixed abode' who, according to your native Babembé legends, caused such harm while they were alive that in death they are turned forever into reptiles of the grave. . .

You could get quite depressed by thoughts like these. But instead you dismiss them with a flick of your hand and do your best to convince yourself this is your new life, it won't be all bad, and soon you'll be heading into town to sort a few things out.

You relax your legs, stretch your arms out in the shape of a cross, and try to release yourself from the protective foetal position you instinctively adopted when the vegetable matter hacked up by earth's eruption and hurled back by the furious cyclone ended up scattered all around you. You crack each of your knuckles in turn, as though an explosion

4

of microbubbles in your joints is irrefutable confirmation of your existence.

Now to check if you can pick things up. You manage to find a small round pebble, like a marble. You roll it between your thumb and index finger, enjoying the relaxing feeling of its touch. Then you close your palm around it and, without getting to your feet, clench your teeth, eyes shut, and hurl it into space.

At first – silence. It feels interminable. Then you hear the little stone bounce several times against the marble of a tombstone three or four rows from yours. You had thrown it way up in the air, no mean feat in itself.

Your lips spread in a broad smile of satisfaction – surely this justifies a resumption of your previous joyful mood, countering the trail of doleful images that lately paraded through your mind.

Refreshed by your wave of euphoria, you finally decide to get up. It's the first time you've stood upright since you emerged from the tomb. Supporting yourself on the wooden cross, you manage somehow to straighten up without breaking it. You ignore the creaking of your elbow joints as you shake the reddish earth from your clothes. You're wearing an orange crepe jacket with wide lapels, a fluorescent-green shirt with a large collar, three buttons and round musketeer cuffs. Your white bow tie is a little askew, so you adjust it, remembering how Mâ Lembé hated it when you wore it off-centre to church. You seem to have got a bit wet here and there; your shirt is a little damp in the armpits, down the back, round your belly. You must have been sweating back there in your casket, you think.

You cast an admiring look at your purple flares, also of crepe, and your shiny red white-laced Salamanders. And since they might restrict your movement, you resolve to slip off your shoes and toss them from your grave, goggling at those elevator heels – after all, you're not exactly lacking in the height department.

You have to admit it: these shoes were a quick sell from some trader near where you work at the Victory Palace. It's a French hotel, close by the Lumumba roundabout, and not far from there is the Grand Marché, where every day Ponte-negrins fall upon the bundles of clothes and boxes of shoes that have been shipped out from France, mostly from Marseille, Bordeaux or Le Havre. Young people have a word for these hand-me-downs – *sola*, which means 'choose' in Munu-kutuba. The clothes arrive in Pointe-Noire packed tight, wrapped in plastic and sealed against theft. The shoes come in tough cloth bags, again tightly sealed. The big-time traders (Lebanese, Senegalese and Maghreb) buy them in bulk and pass them on to the little traders (the Pontenegrins) to sell at retail. Once the bales and bags have been opened and unpacked, the traders place the shoes and clothes in piles on squares of canvas spread out on the ground in the centre of the marketplace. The customers sniff at them like dogs, and try them on, heedless of the people watching them strip off in public. They put their selection to one side, or between their legs, and proceed to payment only after haggling for a considerable reduction, especially if they've found a hanging thread, a missing button, a loose label or a microscopic stain. Who cares if only the buyer can see them; the customer is always right, what matters is what he sees. No price is set in stone, it's all 'negotiable'.

As well as a whiff of *sola* – from the clothes bundles or, a more likely hypothesis, from the shop of your favourite Grand Marché trader, Abdoulaye Walaye – you pick up a stronger smell, of Mananas, a kind of eau de toilette sold in Lebanese shops and often sprinkled on corpses. No one would ever use

Mananas in Pointe-Noire, people would think they were a ghost or that they worked in the cemetery or the morgue.

You don't recall quite when your clothes began to smell like this. But you do know you haven't changed your outfit for close on five days now, which means these are the clothes you were buried in...

World Upside Down

———

NERVOUSLY, YOU TAKE A LOOK about you...

The lingering silence and morning mist put a damper on the delight you've been feeling till now. In fact nothing here seems to have been turned upside down or shaken up quite as you thought: the earth bears no sign of seismic tremor, and you start to think the shock you felt three hours ago, the cyclone sucking you up and flinging you back down on your grave, may just have been the product of your reeling imagination.

Also, getting out of here won't be easy. No one is going to forcibly stop you, but something doesn't feel quite right and you can't just dash out there without taking stock of all the pros and cons, or without listening to the hapless tales of those who've gone before you. As a result you're standing stock still by your gravestone, your arms hanging limp at your side. Opposite you, about three hundred metres away, you notice several paths converging at a great central water fountain. Earlier you were unsure which path to take. One of them, the widest path, the one you were tempted to follow, looks endless, with, at the far end, a minute round house, or rather a kind of little hut with a cross on the top, where a giant crow presides, while others, less imposing, perch on the roof cawing or dozing on one leg.

But more than any of this, what alarms you most is the realisation that you're actually seeing everything upside down, so that your head feels like it's at the bottom and your feet at the top, and the distant hut you can see at the end of the main path is upside down as well. All in all, what you can sense ahead of you is behind you, and what is behind you is actually ahead.

Perhaps it was like that all along, that's why you felt the earthquake and the cyclone, but you were so overjoyed you failed to pay attention and focussed on convincing yourself you were alive, you could breathe, pick up objects, throw stones, when in fact your bearings were not at all what they were before.

Don't rub your eyes, it won't change anything.

The sky? Don't look up for it, it's down there, below.

The earth? Don't look down for it, it's up there now.

The many different paths before you, including the widest, which intrigues you, turn into lines that twist and move, glittering, making circles. They all merge together and you can't see properly; your head starts to hurt, your stomach too. You get more and more dizzy as you see planes flying down below, not above, so that you feel you might crash on top of them. Instinctively you hunch up as they pass. You now know that in order to advance you must retreat; and in order to retreat you must advance. In fact you are less bothered by what is happening up above (that is, beneath your feet) than by the aerial traffic down below (that is, beneath your head). You're not surprised to see your footprints facing backwards, as if your eyes and your feet had fallen out and, in their failure to agree, decided to go their separate ways, without asking for your approval. . .

9

Since you are now finding it hard to lift your feet off the ground, every step demands a Herculean effort, and as soon as you manage to take one, it echoes in your head like an earthquake, reminding you of the moment the earth moved a few hours earlier. But you force yourself to move forward, bearing in mind the chameleon's traditional wisdom, as acquired at primary school in the Trois-Cents district. Monsieur Malonga, your teacher, told you the tale of this reptile, worshipped by the African people. When the chameleon sets off in one direction he never turns his head, just an eye, so as not to lose sight of his goal. When he moves forward, he does so with caution; first he looks up, then down, gathering information before blending into the background.

You can hear your teacher, Malonga, his deep voice, praising the wisdom of the ancestors – a wisdom you need to channel right now to find your way out of here.

You tell yourself: choose a direction, don't turn your head, just your eye; look up, look down, till you find the exit leading to the other side and down into town, so you can go and sort out what's weighing on your heart.

You boost up your courage by muttering: 'I, Liwa Ekimakingaï, am a chameleon, a real chameleon. Oh yes I am. . .'

Alas, unlike the chameleon, who is able to move forward, you find yourself walking round in circles for hours on end, believing, quite wrongly, you've been walking so far that your feet are about to explode. The distance from each grave to the next seems like a chasm. You gasp for breath, though you have no recollection of walking at a great pace, or with a long stride. Your mouth feels dry; you would trade your most precious possession, that is to say your soul, for a glass of fresh water from a limpid stream bordered by trees in blossom, from which the sweet song of new and unknown species of bird meets your ear as you sit on a rock and contemplate in wonder the majestic river's flow and the leaping fish with their iridescent scales.

Whatever you see, and try to approach, retreats with every step you take, and when you think you've reached it the whole thing pops up behind you, when you believed it lay ahead. You look down and notice, to your disappointment, that although you moved around a little bit, you only circled round and round your grave, or round a grave two or three down the line, never more than that, and your wooden cross is still planted there; you're in your stockinged feet, your Salamander shoes are scattered about, your orange crepe jacket with the wide lapels that you dropped is lying there on the ground, and your green fluorescent shirt with the broad collar and round musketeer cuffs is no longer wet under the armpits, or at the back, or above your belly, as the sun has now risen and quickly dried up the dampness, though it has failed to deal with the stubborn stains that look almost like the contours of certain countries of the world, drawn up by a skilful cartographer.

You're still wearing your purple flares, there's still a strong smell of Mananas – but that won't surprise anyone round here.

At first you held the anxiety and exhaustion in check, but now they they're back. You slump down on your grave, in the exact spot earlier where you struggled to your feet. You realise there's no getting ahead of yourself; there are things here beyond your control.

Again you hear the breeze stirring the leaves of a tree. It's a mango you hadn't noticed till now, just by your grave. You should be happy; you're the only one here lucky enough to lie beneath a fruit tree. Leaves and wind together dispense a calming sweetness, as though unseen forces in the air are cradling you, bringing you comfort.

You've grown accustomed to this pleasant sense of indolence, and you start to drift into a deep sleep, unaware that you are now entering upon the longest dream of your death...

As Cormorants Take Flight

––

IMAGES CROWD IN ON YOU in this longest dream of your death. They arise in no particular order, following their own whims and fancies, with an autonomy previously unknown to you in dreams. Images from the four days of your funeral interrupt others from your childhood; images from your adolescence mingle with places in Pointe-Noire, and people, or significant moments from your life.

You feel this immense happiness, no resistance, nothing blocking your way. You stretch out your arms, you take off, flying from one point to another with the ease of an eagle. Yes, it turns out you have wings too, the cormorants having nothing over you now, those birds you admired as a child, flying over the Côte Sauvage, heedless of their weight as they took proudly to the air in elegant flight, and you wondered what you would do one day if you too could fly like some aquatic bird.

And now here you are, flying. You rise higher, and from up here you can see the dilapidated roofs of the poor districts. For a while you follow the twists and turns of the Tchinouka river, bearing its cargo of detritus on to the Atlantic.

You notice buses caught in traffic and pousse-pousses at the busiest junctions in the city. You pass the town centre, studying the colonial architecture that jostles with the chaos of new buildings in the Mouyondzi, Mvoumvou, Kilomètre-Quatre or Mbota districts.

Up, up and up you fly, then descend with the grace of those cormorants from your childhood to the Trois-Cents district where you used to live.

People are spread out all around you, clapping. You are moved by this welcome for your landing, the more so as it comes with compliments attached:

'Bravo, Liwa Ekimakingaï! Bravo!'

'You fly like Superman!'

'How does it feel up there?'

You've come to rest; your arms fall back by your sides. Your wings retract beneath your shoulders. You know now that if you just raise your arms up high and flap them a few times your wings will reappear and you'll take off.

You greet the group applauding you. You wander round the streets of the Trois-Cents district where other people wave to you from the doorways of their plots or from balconies. Some ask where you've been since yesterday. You went off into the forest for a rest, you say; now you're on your way home, your grandmother, Mâ Lembé, is waiting for you. Some invite you in for a bite to eat, a drink. You refuse their invitations; you're sorry, you say, next time. You explain that Mâ Lembé's worried; she hasn't seen you since the night of Independence Day, 15 August, over five days ago. You see the disappointment in their faces, you apologise once again and continue on your way.

You've been walking for over thirty minutes now, and are concerned you haven't yet found the road that leads to the house where you've always lived. In theory it should only have taken about ten minutes. You know for sure that your street is the one where the Joli-Soir dance bar is, or rather that the bar is to be found in this street, so if you can locate it your old home will be very close by.

Swallowing your pride – it's ridiculous, surely, to ask for help – you ask some young people playing draughts in front of a plot where the house is half-built but already inhabited.

You've scarcely said hello and they're already shrieking in horror:

'Help! Help! Help!'

They abandon their game and leg it, leaving you standing there stupefied by their reaction.

You go back the way you came, convinced these young folk – some of them your own age – are cretins of the first order who devote their lives to indolence and leisure.

You come to the place where you landed earlier to great applause. You can still hear the emotion in those voices as they watched you descend from on high and fold up your wings.

Alas, many of the individuals who cheered you then, chanting your name, also take to their heels when you approach. Four of them stay, though, like they're looking for a confrontation. They're walking purposefully towards you now. Their bodies are human, but each has the head of a different animal: a hyena, a shrew, an orangutang and a white shark.

'Go back to Frère-Lachaise!' one of the men cries, the one with the white shark's head.

The one with the orangutang head chimes in:

'Yes, back home with you!'

Shrew Man pipes up:

'You're frightening the children, the dogs are going crazy!'

Hyena Man is categorical, not to say threatening:

'If you don't turn back now you'll die a second time!'

Though they're shaking sticks at you, ready to strike, your reply is conciliatory:

'Come on, guys, you've made a mistake; we met earlier. I'm looking for the rue du Joli-Soir. I just want to find my house, I'm really tired, please let me through. . .'

'Get out of here! Go and join your own kind!' they all shout in chorus, getting more and more aggressive.

Now it's your turn to take off like someone who's stolen fruit and vegetables at the Grand Marché, with these ogres flinging their sticks after you, clearly loving every minute of it.

You come to the top of an empty patch of land, far from everything, and try to redeploy your wings and take flight. This time, though, nothing comes out from your shoulder blades. You must keep walking along the avenue de l'Indépendance, trusting your intuition, hoping it doesn't steer you back to those horrible people who chased you with their sticks of wood.

You're still pretty confident; surely you'll find the Trois-Cents district in the end, and the rue du Joli-Soir. . .

Tastes Like Mood Balls

———

YOU WERE RIGHT TO KEEP WALKING directly down the avenue de l'Indépendence, which runs perpendicular to the rue du Joli-Soir.

You're now right outside the dance bar. Your grandmother's house is only three plots on from here, and the café's closed right now. It always closes when someone local dies. It allows the bar owner both to honour the deceased and avoid disturbing the funeral celebrations by creating an overly competitive atmosphere between those who are having a great time dancing for joy and those who sing and weep in sorrow.

You stand there, outside your plot, intrigued to see so many people packed together inside. From a distance you can just see your own body lying under a canopy of palm leaves with tearful women of a certain age standing all around. You don't like the look of this, and you refuse to believe that the vigil is for the corpse of your good self, Liwa Ekimakingaï. You'd really like to just go to your room and have a rest. But for that you would have to make your way through the kind and sympathetic crowd who have turned out to support your grandmother in her grief.

You can't do that; you've exceeded the number of times, according to Babembé legend, that a dead person can see themselves. In theory it's only possible twice. Which means you can't be in your death bed under this canopy and in Frère-Lachaise dreaming the longest dream of your death *and* also want to shut yourself away in your childhood room while all these people in your house are showing support for your grandmother.

You catch odd bits of conversation. The women round your corpse congratulate your grandmother on owning property 'without a man's help'. You bring your gaze to rest on the wood-built house, which seems even smaller in your dream, angled slightly towards the street, as though peering at what is going on over at the Joli-Soir. And yet that's where you lived your whole life, one of those rooms was yours. The iron sheeting on the roof needs replacing. You'd promised to deal with it, you haven't done it yet; it lets in rain water and in the dry season swallows and swifts build their nests between the rafters.

Since you can't be in three different places at once you abandon the idea of hiding out in your room; instead you stand there like a pillar of salt, while in your mind's eye scenes from your childhood jostle for position, including several memorable ones from Joli-Soir. So you turn back in that direction, fascinated by the constant flow of people arriving at your house. Before long the people coming to the wake will fill up most of the street.

To you, the rue du Joli-Soir is the most beautiful street in all the world. You can buy kebabs here, made from chicken and mutton. The air smells of 'mood balls', dough balls leavened with yeast. The smell of them, a good smell, wipes out the vision of the corpse in the middle of your plot, awakens the only child you once were, who wandered through the streets of this town and ran barefoot along the Côte Sauvage with his shirt flapping open; who always came home in time, just as the one person in all the world he cared for, Mâ Lembé, had finished making his favourite dish of beans and salt fish, with a side of manioc leaves.

But in your dream the dish tastes different: the fish isn't at all salty and the beans are spoilt, the manioc leaves served up in a clumsy heap. No, Mâ Lembé can't have made this, she'd never have got it so wrong. And it hasn't come from the restaurants down by the River Tchinouka either; they'd lose all their customers. You have no choice; you eat, you eat the mood balls with it, and notice the aftertaste of eggs mixed with flour, milk, sugar and butter. The dough balls are sold by Beninese women who settled in the town in the 1960s. Mâ Lembé used to send you to buy some or go herself, as a treat if you'd worked hard at school – and in that she was never disappointed: you were one of the best pupils at the primary school in the Trois-Cents. Sometimes, too, she would buy you mood balls if you'd behaved impeccably towards the elderly and helped them cross the road, or find their way home, or chased off the mangey and scabby dogs, barking fiercely with bared teeth as they went by.

As you're taken back to childhood by your meal with the mood balls, even though it lacks the authentic flavour of Mâ Lembé's cooking, you find yourself sitting on a bench at school, in the middle row, squashed between two of your friends, José Manuel Lopes and Sosthène Mboma. You'd been inseparable since primary school, and your families knew each other.

José Manuel Lopes's parents were originally from the enclave of Cabinda and took up exile in Pointe-Noire when Angola annexed their territory, which was rich in petrol and much coveted by the major European powers. Papa Lopes was a militant resistant in the Liberation Front of the State of Cabinda. The members of this opposition were hunted down and had mostly fled Cabinda. In the district he was known not by his own name but as 'the Opposer'. Calm of manner, with big intellectual-type glasses, he generally wore a desert jacket and a cap with a motif of Che Guevara or a big red star.

José had two younger sisters, Lesliana and Ana Clara, both born in Pointe-Noire, whose parents used to joke that they weren't Cabindi, they were Congolese. The children helped their father post up tracts around town showing unbearable images of Cabindi people who had been abused by the Angolan regime, or even executed, with the intention of intimidating the opposition and the symbolic Cabindi government over in Europe which Angola, naturally enough, rejected, expecting the international community to do the same.

The Mboma family, on the other hand, came from Oyo, in the north of the country. Papa Mboma worked for the Congo–Ocean Railway on the Pointe-Noire-to-Brazzaville route, while Maman Mboma, who declared herself a 'housewife', single-handedly cared for their only son, Sosthène, as the father was constantly travelling. Papa Mboma was known in the district as 'the northerner'; people wondered if being sent to work in the south hadn't been a sort of banishment, since the northerners governed the country. He could actually have lived in Brazzaville and used the fact that he was a northerner to secure a political position. But he didn't give a damn about that; he had loved the railways and trains since he was a child. He even collected miniature locomotives, which Sosthène would show you in secret.

'If he finds me touching his trains he'll string me up!' your friend warned.

Sosthène would tell you the names of all the different models of miniature trains; the engines that ran on diesel, others on steam, or the electric ones produced by Jouef or Vespa, bearing the logo of the French railways, the SNCF.

In the north of the country there are no trains; there isn't even a railway. Papa Mboma had realised his dream and passed the entrance exam for the Congo–Ocean Railway. He was quite sure he would work in the south, and one year after taking up the position he fell for the charms of a southern woman, Maman Mboma, with whom he would have a child, your pal Sosthène.

The Lopes and Mboma families had immense respect for your grandmother. Maman Lopes and Maman Mboma would stop and say hello to Mâ Lembé at the Grand Marché. The three of them talked about everything, especially the behaviour of their children, then they promised they'd all meet up back in the neighbourhood, but since their houses were some way apart these promises were never fulfilled and sadly they mostly only met up for the wrong reasons: if your trio was being talked about, and complaints were starting to build up. . .

Death Was Afraid of Me

———

YOU, JOSÉ AND SOSTHÈNE were inseparable all through your adolescence. You quickly got the upper hand with your two classmates, not because you were a year older, but because from primary school onwards you told them stories which they listened to attentively, never batting an eyelid, even when they were quite sure you were taking them for a ride, adding a touch of salt or spice here and there to keep their attention.

Whenever you went to school all together they'd meet you at the end of the rue du Joli-Soir, each with an almost identical backpack – your parents bought them from the same Lebanese shop at the Grand Marché – and you'd set off down the avenue de l'Indépendence to walk over two hours to the communist secondary school, the Trois-Glorieuses, at the intersection of the Avenues Jacques-Opangault and Amílcar-Cabral.

You loved geography, learning about distant places you dreamed you would visit when you were grown up. However, unlike José, you hated history – all those dates to remember. He was an enthusiast for it – probably because of his father's experience. His father must have talked to his children at table or at bedtime about the tragic fate of Cabinda.

Like Sosthène, you were pretty good at spelling and dictation. To help you with your homework – and also to gain inspiration for the stories you'd tell your friends – you devoured books you borrowed from the Charles-Miningou library in the central Mouyondzi district. Every year Mâ Lembé paid your subscription to the library and was reassured if she knew you were there, that you weren't wandering about by the Tchinouka river with your two partners in crime. The Chinese had built the library and provided books from all over the world. They wanted to help a fellow country emerge from ignorance, as you were taught to say in citizenship classes. Several high-school students were sent to Beijing, where they continued their studies, returning later to hold important posts in government or on the Central Committee of the Congolese Workers' Party, the CWP. . .

You could have gone on studying past the general first certificate, which you obtained with ease at the communist college of the Trois-Glorieuses. But you had to curb the thirst for knowledge that had drawn you from the Trois-Cents to the Charles-Miningou library, where you devoured *The Adventures of Tom Sawyer*, the little American whose tribulations you would later relate dramatically to José and Sosthène. You believed that the fictional town of St Petersburg – where the little American Tom Sawyer lived, supposedly somewhere on the River Mississippi in the state of Missouri – was a real place, the sister town to Pointe-Noire. You imagined the River Mississippi as a cousin to the Atlantic Ocean at Pointe-Noire.

Ever intent on displaying your passion for this bedside read, from which you could recite entire chapters without stumbling over a single word, you cast yourself as Tom Sawyer – he too was an orphan, and was raised by his aunt Polly, as you were by your grandmother. And as if this similarity wasn't enough, you felt the need to surround yourself with friends of the same name. So you gave José the nickname 'Huckleberry Finn' and Sosthène that of 'Joe Harper'.

These names were not chosen at random: Sosthène was pretty much your favourite, as Joe Harper was Tom Sawyer's. You liked the same things. He was prepared to follow you blindly, while José Manuel Lopes, like Huckleberry Finn, dreamed of building a raft, to escape from Pointe-Noire and leave his parents' rows behind, especially those of his father, who drank from morning till night and unleashed his wrath on his family, usually in public. In the neighbourhood they attributed this behaviour to the worsening political situation: the installation by Angola of an impressive military presence in the enclave of Cabinda had such a profound effect on Papa Lopes that he sought comfort in alcohol.

No, you would never have set foot on José's raft, you wanted to stay close to Mâ Lembé. At which point he would have asked Sosthène 'Joe Harper' to join him. The two of them would have played a game of pirates and warm-hearted bandits, like Robin Hood, another character you were all fascinated by, because he looked out for the poor and oppressed – like the people of Cabinda, José would add. Whereupon Sosthène would suggest to José that they attack the trains of the Chemin de Fer Congo–Océan and distribute the goods they seized to the people of the villages.

Either way, the two adventurers would have travelled by the River Tchinouka. They'd have ended up as young soldiers in the rebellion in far-off Cabinda, hiding out in the maquis, ready to take up arms the moment they got the signal from the commander of the opposition, who'd recruited them to liberate this rich enclave from the clutches of Angola.

It was down to you that most of the group's crazy ideas and tricks were inspired by *The Adventures of Tom Sawyer*. But your gang went further – Tom Sawyer wasn't a bad lad, after all. Lazy, maybe, eager for recognition, but with a fertile imagination, which eventually earned him more gratitude than he probably deserved. But in your case, the mark had been overstepped. There were more and more complaints, and soon enough the local leaders became aware of them. Your parents were at their wits' end, their reprimands and punishments having no effect at all.

Occasionally Mâ Lembé paid the fines at the Trois-Cents police station, dragging you along with her with your head hung low, pulling your ears in front of the officers. One time someone complained that you and your gang had trashed Monsieur Kibandi's garden, then stolen mangoes from Monsieur Bilampassi's fields, over by Agostinho Neto Airport. Another that you'd stolen tyres off Monsieur Masseongo's bike, and sold them to Monsieur Kikadidi. Yet another time that you'd dropped a banana skin outside the shop of Diamoucoune, the Senegalese, and laughed when the poor man skidded on it.

You had by now acquired a reputation for your varied bag of tricks, some of them bordering on petty criminality. Some people simply called you 'bandits', or 'hoodlums', or 'delinquents'. You were the head of operations, the brains; the others were the rest of the body, the limbs, blindly carrying out your plans.

As a last resort, Mâ Lembé evoked your mother's memory:

'If Albertine was alive today she would not be proud of you!'

She added that Albertine was not at all happy over there in the other world, where she must be thinking she, Mâ Lembé, had failed to keep the promise she had made to her in the Adolphe-Cissé hospital: to help you to become an honourable man. The doctor had just told her that Albertine had died from complications of childbirth. Mâ Lembé suddenly realised that from now on she would be both mother and grandmother to you.

Somewhat unoriginally, she decided to call you 'Liwa Ekimakingaï', meaning 'Death was afraid of me'. At first she wanted to call you Yezu Christo, but the city authorities refused flat out, pointing out that there was only one Jesus Christ in this world, and it was forbidden to take his name in vain. To do so would be to put the child in evil odour, making a hell of his life here below.

In fact the name Liwa Ekimakingaï suited you: through it you became proof that Albertine was alive, that she had breathed her life into yours, a life eternal. You only ever saw features of your mother in the black and white photos that Mâ Lembé showed you. As a small child, you loved to sit on her knee as she leafed through an old photo album. You'd look long and hard at the young woman, whose eyes sparkled with life. This was Albertine. This was your mother. . .

'She was so beautiful. . .'

You said this to Mâ Lembé not because Albertine was your mother but because she had taken everything from your grandmother while she herself was in the prime of life. Those fine facial features, the graceful neck with sparkling jewels of ebony and sometimes ivory. . .

Yes, she was tall. You're one metre ninety yourself, and get your height from her. Mâ Lembé, who is ten centimetres shorter than you, was always saying so.

'Liwa, you're the same height as your mother. When I see you, it's like I'm seeing her.'

The Policeman

———

MÂ LEMBÉ IS OMNIPRESENT in your dream.

You hear her telling you she was not far off forty when she had your mother, Albertine, in Mouyondzi, in the Bouenza region, a southern part of the country you have never set foot in – why would she take you back to the place where, in her view, all her troubles began? Your grandfather, whom you never knew – she would not have wanted you to – was a policeman, and had recently been transferred to that region to work at the magistrates' court. Mâ Lembé met him there for the first time the day she went to complain about her neighbours' son who had stolen one of her goats and sold it. The policeman posted at the entrance to the building was charged with checking identity cards. After examining Mâ Lembé's document at some length he whispered to her quietly that she reminded him of his cousin in Madoungou, up in the north of Mouyondzi. Mâ Lembé simply smiled, more concerned with getting her complaint heard and receiving swift compensation from her neighbours. She was wearing a light-weight orange blouse over a pair of very tight trousers made of electric-green jersey. Her yellow high-heeled shoes rang out with every step she took. She went on her way, unaware that behind her the policeman was staring fixedly at her arse as she advanced down the corridor towards the desk to wait her turn.

A dozen or so plaintiffs were ahead of her.

She turned around and caught the policeman signalling to his colleague at the desk that he should move your grandmother up to the front of the queue. Why would she not accept, if for once she could skip the lengthy administration everyone complained of?

Mâ Lembé was extremely pleased: the policeman promised to send an officer to 'intimidate' the neighbours into paying for her goat 'in five seconds flat'.

Her benefactor showed up that very evening at Mâ Lembé's house. Power and the general fear inspired by his police uniform afforded him the liberty to do so.

So what happened that evening? Your grandmother was pretty tight-lipped about this, conceding only that:

'I made the biggest mistake of my life... But having said that, it was a mistake that gave me a reason to live: your mother. And now, it's you... I never heard from the policeman again, once I told him he was going to be a father...'

She paused for breath then continued:

'He was ashamed to have made a child with me; in his eyes I was just some old woman...'

The whole of Mouyondzi talked of nothing but 'the woman who got knocked up by the policeman', and your grandmother was accused of having been determined to have a child with this man for economic reasons. In the end Mâ Lembé tired of the constant humiliating talk of the women, and even of the men – who dubbed her 'the policeman's easy lay' – and decamped overnight from Mouyondzi to Pointe-Noire, taking little Albertine with her.

The Little Chief with the Big Scar

———

IN A YEAR YOUR GRANDMOTHER had acquired a patch of land in the Trois-Cents and built a wooden house on it. She was able to do this thanks to the women of the Grand Marché, whose solidarity was no myth.

As soon as she arrived she heard talk of a certain Sabine Bouanga, an elderly woman who was both the most respected and most feared of women at the Grand Marché. It was impossible to find a stand there without going via Sabine Bouanga, and she brooked no resistance to her influence.

Things were less complicated for Mâ Lembé as Sabine Bouanga, like her, came from the Bouenza region and was of Babembé descent. There was a tribal aspect to the market, at least when it came to trade in certain products. Accordingly, Sabine Bouanga was said to have generated not only tribal leanings in the market, but also a certain prejudice in favour of women. Women dominated its principal activities, specialising in the sale of palm oil, fruit and vegetables, manioc, tobacco, rice, salt, smoked and salted fish, letting the men get on with selling wood, charcoal, bread and meat.

In spite of the significant presence of the women there, it

was still the men who called the shots from the Mairie, and Sabine Bouanga knew them all. She was the only one they were afraid of, and no one forgot the day she was refused a stand for one of her childhood friends from Bouenza. She turned up furious to see the head of the Market department at the Mairie and the scene that ensued is etched into the memory of all Pontenegrins.

'So you're refusing my childhood friend a table? Very well, let's settle things here and now. We'll soon see who wears the trousers!' she threatened.

She took off her clothes and bellowed like a mad cow, aiming her bare arse at the Mairie officials.

'There you are – get an eyeful of that!'

The general commotion reached its peak when she spread her legs and released a torrential stream of urine that continued to flow till Zacharie Gampion, known as 'the little chief with the big scar', intervened. His face had been scarred when he was born, like many of the Batékés. Scarification, he maintained, was part of their concept of Beauty. Zacharie Gampion responded to any detractors by marginalising another section of the population, though those listening often didn't get the point of his comparisons:

'The cheeks of those without scars are as boring as a pygmy's bottom! I was lucky to receive the blessing of my Téké ancestors, who are actually the only ones who can lay claim to land ownership in this country. We're not like the rest of you – we're from the north and the south; you'll find us in Gabon as well as the two Congos!'

That day, to calm Sabine Bouanga down, the little chief with the big scar promised her the Mairie would give her friend a stand and would charge only half the usual fee for the licence in the first year.

Then he turned to his staff and declared:

'She's the boss of the Grand Marché, not me! She knows what goes on there. I'm just there to fix the administration!'

This final remark assured Sabine she was held in high esteem. While she was putting her clothes back on, the crowd turned their backs to her, for fear of being cursed. They all knew that the ancestors and traditions showed no mercy: if you didn't look away when an angry mama exposed her naked body you'd never be the same; bad luck would follow you all the days of your life.

The little chief with the big scar knew this too; he had a healthy respect for tradition and had no wish to lose his job over some argument about a table.

So the market women had a reputation for all helping one another. They paid a monthly subscription agreed to by everyone, and each of them in turn was given the money in strict order of rotation. As there were about a hundred of them and each of them undertook to contribute 50,000 CFA francs a month, Mâ Lembé had pocketed over five million, a sum she could never in her life have got together in such record time. Back then the five million francs easily covered the purchase of a piece of land in the rue du Joli-Soir in the Trois-Cents neighbourhood.

Even when someone received their big payment, they had to carry on paying the subscription, till the very last tradeswoman had had her turn. It was known as the *Likelemba*, a system of interest-free credit founded on decency, word of honour, mutual trust and genuine friendship. Sabine Bouanga made sure everyone kept their word. Anyone tempted to play dirty risked losing their place at the market. As a result no one had ever been known to abuse the system, and at the end of the month Sabine Bouanga visited each woman's stand to collect her dues.

Mâ Lembé was able to buy her plot in the rue du Joli-Soir because so many people from Bouenza and the Babembé tribe had also built their houses there. The purchase price took account of the purchaser's line of descent, so she had a bit left over to build her house of wood.

What became your room had previously been your mother's. . .

Demons in White Blouses

———

ONCE ALBERTINE REACHED ADOLESCENCE Mâ Lembé stopped counting the number of times she had to shoo away what she called the 'grown-up cockerels' forcing their attentions on her in the district. Among the young lady's admirers were fathers, traditional leaders, civil servants, notorious polygamists promising to pay a dowry Mâ Lembé could scarcely refuse. Some of them ambushed the girl while she was out running errands for her mother, and handed her notes. Mâ Lembé reported them to the police. The police retorted that Albertine was a tease; she ought to stop wearing short skirts and 'T-shirts that excite people in the street, showing off her two biggest assets'. Some policemen even insulted her indirectly with the repellent expression 'like mother like daughter...'

To warn her daughter of the dangers waiting for her out there, your grandmother drew on her own experiences with the policeman she never named:

'Men are such lowlifes! They're happy to shoot their load at night, then in the day they run off from their responsibilities like squirrels smelling smoke in the bush.'

After all this time she still could not swallow her anger, and added:

'Especially policemen! There's nothing you can do, they're protected by their colleagues. They filed my complaint and buried it, and to this day I don't know where they posted the imbecile that fathered you!'

She wanted your mother to pursue her studies 'to give those policemen a kick up the arse', she'd insist, as though to transmit to her daughter her contempt for these state employees, but Albertine wanted to be a trader at the Grand Marché, like her.

In the end Mâ Lembé agreed, and found her a stall alongside her own. And right up to when you were born she sold beauty products bought in bulk from the West Africans in the Rex Quarter, an arrangement that worked very well...

Albertine had just turned eighteen when Mâ Lembé detected her body was becoming 'that of a woman'. This metamorphosis was more than just the usual transition from adolescence to adulthood. Mâ Lembé knew her daughter was pregnant but she put off confronting her, feeling it was up to her to confide in her mother. This conversation would never take place, though signs of the pregnancy became increasingly evident: the vomiting, weight gain, giddiness and mood swings.

Mâ Lembé realised Albertine would never admit anything. And indeed, she would leave this life without ever divulging the identity of her child's father.

The circumstances of Albertine's death stupefied the doctors. They hadn't seen a case like hers for decades. Medicine, they maintained, had made progress.

Your mother had lost too much blood. Cup after cupful. The doctors used technical terms, spoke of 'post-partum haemorrhage'. Broadly speaking, they explained to Mâ Lembé, Albertine had lost too much blood right after giving birth, which nowadays almost never happened. Your grand-mother was dubious about this and accused them straight out of lying, in their 'crude French designed for covering up sorcery that in any case they'd learned all wrong from the whites'.

Indeed, she had her own explanation, and this was the one that her friends at the Grand Marché held on to: Albertine had not died from the loss of blood – harmful spirits and envious souls and maybe the bad karma of her wicked progenitor killed her, aided and abetted by the doctors at the Adolphe-Cissé hospital.

She said to them:

'Also, when I saw the doctors, they didn't even look like normal human beings, if you know what I mean. I swear to you they were demons in white blouses, tasked with stealing my daughter's soul and taking it back to their chief, down in hell! If I'd known that at the outset, I'd have left for Mouyondzi with Albertine, and she could have given birth in the bush with the help of a midwife from among my people!'

The assembly of women were in agreement with this, and all chanted in chorus:

'Yes, Mâ Lembé, you're so right!'

And you, too, would live with this suspicion. One day you were convinced your mother had lost her life to a haemorrhage, the next you blamed the supposed witchcraft of the hospital personnel.

And just as Albertine had never known her father, you would never know yours. . .

'Thanks Be to God'

———

THE SCENE APPEARING NOW in your dream comes from before you were ten years old. Back then, to guide you towards what she considered the right path, Mâ Lembé had sought the support of the Pentecostal church Thanks Be to God. She had no idea that just as you were about to receive baptism, she would have cause to regret a decision which had consequences that still astound you to this day...

On Sundays Mâ Lembé would dress in white with a green head scarf, and you'd put on a black suit made by the local tailor, Maître Sivory, who also made your school uniform.

Sunday ritual was respected: very early in the morning, having sent you to quickly 'wash off the stain of your sins in the shower', and, after that, authorised you to go into her room, she would open a metal trunk and take out your 'Thanks Be to God' suit, dressing you with an attention to detail you would never forget, especially making sure your white bow tie wasn't loose, or askew. Many years later you still had the tic of hitching it up even when it was perfectly in place.

As soon as she had finished helping you get dressed, she would chivvy you, saying:

'Come on, let's go, or we'll be late for seven o' clock mass, and God can't abide latecomers. Don't you go believing people who say the last will be first in the Kingdom of Heaven, I'd rather be first come first served...'

She pressed on ahead of you till you came to the avenue de l'Indépendence, where you took a bus from outside Studio-Photo Ndzo-Boni station.

Thanks Be to God Church, in the Rex district, was a kind of giant shack, but it was solidly built, with corrugated iron instead of straw and a poured-concrete floor painted blue. The metal chairs were fixed to the floor and painted green. This place of worship could hold over a thousand people and when there were even more than that, especially when they had a special speaker, people spilled out to pray in the street and listen to mass through loudspeakers.

When you arrived at Thanks Be to God you said hello to the sisters and brothers in Christ in the entrance discussing verses from the Bible – their way of demonstrating their faith. Mâ Lembé would meet up with some of her friends from the Grand Marché, including the influential Sabine Bouanga who had persuaded most of her colleagues to join Thanks Be to God. They talked in Bembé while you stayed in your corner, intimidated to find yourself in the midst of such a pious congregation, but disinclined to join the group of kids over there clustered on one side, even though Mâ Lembé urged you to.

'Go see the other children, chat with them about kids' things!'

No, you'd rather stay with her and her friends, even though you hated the suffocating smell of mothballs from the new *pagnes* the women only brought out of the trunk for Sundays. Every time you smelled it, you were transported back to church and the women's multicoloured *pagnes*, made out of fabric that cost a fortune, particularly the waxed ones, imported from countries in West Africa. Besides, the richest sellers from the market are the women who sell the *pagnes*; you see them driving around in their brand-new luxury cars, that's why they get called 'Mama Benz'...

When the bell pealed for the start of mass, Mâ Lembé would take your hand and you would go in and sit down in the front row, as though the Lord might overlook the people sitting at the back.

Kids clothed in green went round handing out candles, and you had to light them straight away. Then you'd hear music coming from the out-of-tune organ, accompanied by the sound of tam-tams being played frenetically by four young people ripped like Beninese fishermen, their faces smeared with pale clay. They looked like robots, with their shaved heads, silent as sphinxes. Their eyes began to glow as soon as the women's choir started singing, soon to be joined by the lower voices of the men.

Mâ Lembé began to quiver and shake; she 'felt' the Holy Spirit within her and yelled in a guttural voice:

'Thank you, Lord! Thank you, Lord! Thank you, Lord!'

As the crowd clapped their hands you waited in vain for a similar communion with God. The rejoicing went on till the trance had spread throughout the church interior, till finally there appeared, through a hidden door of the shack, in a column of thick red smoke, the long-awaited one, the envoy of the Holy Spirit to Pointe-Noire, a bald, friendly-looking pastor known as 'Papa Bonheur'.

At his approach the faithful started speaking 'in tongues', a sort of mumbo jumbo you could make no sense of, but which, everyone assured you, came from Heaven. Your grandmother comforted you, urged patience; the Holy Spirit would surely visit you eventually, as he had the rest of the congregation. As far as she was concerned, you were still just a lost soul in the clutches of a wicked world, at the mercy of the Devil.

Papa Bonheur

———

PAPA BONHEUR WAS A SCRAP of a man of around sixty, very
dark-skinned, with slightly protruding eyes.

Mâ Lembé had boundless respect and reverence for him,
as indeed did all the other members of Thanks Be to God, and
your grandmother was convinced he was the one who would
help you steer towards Good, and reject Evil in all its guises.

He claimed he was a direct descendant of the vast kingdom
of Loango which once covered all the territories of Cabinda,
Angola, both Congos and Gabon. He was careful to make it
clear to his detractors that democracy already existed back
in the kingdom of his ancestors, where – unlike in certain
adjoining countries – power was not handed down by succession. If anyone contradicted him or said that power, in the
kingdom of Loango, was actually handed down from uncle to
nephew, which was also a form of succession, Papa Bonheur
would reply in a calm voice:

'As in many African societies, the kingdom of my ancestors
was founded on a system of matriarchy, the pillar of which
was the mother. It is therefore normal that the nephew, the
son of the sister of a king, should occupy a leading role. Don't

forget that the nephew only succeeded the sovereign after being duly elected by an assembly of worthies! Furthermore, the new sovereign had to take part in a mystical initiation ceremony, after which he finally received the status of Mâ Loango, in other words, monarch of the kingdom of Loango!

You had to read between the lines to realise Papa Bonheur also believed himself to be a 'Mâ Loango', even though no assembly had agreed on this and the kingdom whose virtues he was extolling was purely symbolic, since the powers that be did not recognise it as an official institution.

Papa Bonheur was not wrong, though, to insist on the distinction of his ancestors. He was in fact the nephew of one of the last kings of Loango, a fact he liked to make known through his affected manners, his way of delighting in the respects paid to him by the faithful of Thanks Be to God. He was famous for his hand-made suits from Europe, which Mâ Lembé would describe to you with relish after each Sunday service, and he drove a new jeep, which, according to some, was the perfect conveyance for getting him to highly deprived districts, to help street children. He liked to say that the vehicle belonged to the church, that anyone in the congregation might drive it, should they feel the need. But who would ever have dared ask him for the keys to it for their personal use? It was held that the church belonged to the faithful and the Holy Spirit had chosen Papa Bonheur as their protector.

He was considered one of the most honourable people in our town. Even though the existence of Loango was not recognised by the State, the pastor got his revenge when the President of the Republic, visiting the city, paid his respects to him in person before receiving ambassadors from abroad. To Papa Bonheur this indicated recognition of the kingdom of his ancestors and, by inference, of his church. It never occurred to him that the president visited him simply to get the inhabitants of Pointe-Noire to vote for him in the approaching elections. Inside the church you could see photos of him with the Head of State.

Mâ Lembé swore that Thanks Be to God had taken thousands of orphans off the streets, found them homes, and ensured they were cared for till they came of legal age. She told you the story of how the postman-turned-man-of-God had left his position when the Lord bumped into him on the Côte Sauvage, where he'd gone quite unaware that he'd been led there by the Holy Spirit, away from the ungodly, to be assigned the difficult task of purifying the lost sheep of Pointe-Noire. The very day of this great revelation, the postman went back home, demolished his house and built the church in its place, using his own savings and the money the National Postal Service gave him for taking voluntary redundancy.

This initiative led the neighbours to call him a crank, and his wife, who disagreed with his project, left him and took their seven children back to her native village.

To start with, Papa Bonheur's services were principally directed at street children he recruited himself outside cinemas – the Rex, the Roy and Duo. After a few months several of these kids became respectable, well-dressed people, fervent servants of the Lord. Their parents now attended the church too, and expressed their thanks to their leader through donations which grew bigger by the day.

After a while Papa Bonheur started to cruise round different parts of town in search of more lost adolescents, so that before long he was known not as 'le Père Makaya' or 'Pastor Makaya', but rather, in recognition of his great goodness, 'Papa Bonheur' – he who brings joy to ordinary folk. As their congregations started to defect to the newcomer, the other churches in town, which had until then been dismissive of Papa Bonheur's work, began to worry. There was now a huge canteen in front of Thanks Be to God, generously stocked by

Sabine Bouanga and the tradeswomen of the Grand Marché. Anyone could just turn up at meal times and eat as much as they wanted without paying a single CFA franc.

Deep down the pastor believed he was recreating the lost kingdom, and that he could have been its leader if only the government had restored his reputation instead of disgracing him. He had become one of the most important people in the city, especially since the faithful had started to report experiences of his healing the sick by the laying-on of hands.

Papa Bonheur was the last resort of people whom official medicine had failed to cure. How often people of Pointe-Noire took the sick to him, rather than the Adolphe-Cissé hospital! With fake modesty he would remind them that first they should consult the 'whites' hospital' – if they couldn't bring about a recovery, then God would intervene.

With the money given by the faithful he bought a piece of land next to the church, built an annexe for instruction in the Word of God, and even set up catch-up lessons for children who had missed out on school. Volunteer teachers taught Sunday School after mass. You didn't need catch-up lessons; what you needed was the Word of God, Mâ Lembé told you.

People liked to say that you only had to ask for something, the pastor would have a word with God and you were bound to get it.

The day Papa Bonheur first spoke directly to you, you thought you would pass out. The Man of God was standing right in front of you, smiling broadly. Instinctively you closed your eyes, so the words about to fall from his lips might impregnate you fully. These words would descend from on high, immaculate, intended for you, that your soul might be cleansed of the stain between you and redemption. You then heard that hoarse but reassuring voice call you 'my son', and it really felt as though you were standing before your father, he who would deliver you from all evil. The pastor spoke slowly, with a slight pause between each word. This time the Holy Spirit was truly about to enter into you.

But nothing seemed to be happening, though the pastor laid his hand on your head and stroked it for several minutes. Mâ Lembé, who was following the scene with close attention, explained later that it was your lack of faith that had stopped you perceiving the good Lord's plan for you. You must believe, and believe utterly; that was the only way to get remission of sins and come into the presence of God. Once you spoke in tongues, like the rest of the faithful, you could at last be plunged into water and receive baptism in the Holy Spirit, which was in great demand, and publicly declare your commitment to walk with Jesus.

'Once you've been baptised you'll be a true child of God,' she would say, as you were walking home.

You needed to show even more commitment.

So you helped the cooks at Thanks Be to God, you handed out meals to the hundreds of children who turned up outside the church at midday. You accompanied some of the brothers in Christ to public squares and bars to announce the Good News. It was no sinecure; people would turn away, tell you to clear off or, worse still, throw chilli water in your face. They couldn't care less about Paradise, the flames of Gehenna held no fears for them. They laughed in your face when you reminded them the end of the world was nigh.

Meanwhile, Papa Bonheur was spreading his church's aura internationally. Other pastors arrived, from Brazil, Nigeria, Ghana or the United States, to meet him in person.

The arrival in Pointe-Noire of pastor Steve Simpson, a black American, was a huge event at Thanks Be to God. No one in

43

our town had ever heard a man of God preach so eloquently. The entire straw building rang with the American's voice; you could hear it throughout the neighbourhood. You would find him at the Patrice Lumumba roundabout, standing on a stool. Addressing the crowd. Even though he spoke in English, and no one understood a word, the Pontenegrins flocked to see him and shout 'Amen!'

Pastor Aje Tanimol, on the other hand, was quite different. He brought with him from Nigeria a terrifying statuette that was treated like a real person. It moved to the rhythm of the tam-tam, nodded its head whenever the Nigerian pastor started to pray and scowled with rage when people disturbed its master's mass with chatter. The pastor only spoke Yoruba, and his red eyes protruded from their sockets when he went into a trance. He and Papa Bonheur went out every evening to the Côte Sauvage to talk with the spirits that rose up from the briny depths and remained with them till sunrise.

Mâ Lembé was proud to inform you that Papa Bonheur was also invited abroad. The faithful would meet him at the airport and the long procession would then return on foot to the church, where the pastor would recount all that he had learned on his travels. He came back radicalised, excoriating certain passages in the Bible, saying the holy book contained no black angels or apostles, even though, in his view, people of colour had been around before any of the other races, and everyone, whites included, agreed that Africa was the cradle of humanity.

His rebukes set the loudspeakers crackling:

'The whites stole our spirituality! They put ridiculous apostles in the Bible, in our place! Let us gird our loins and announce to all the world that God is black; those images they sell showing a white-skinned Jesus are heresy, a distortion of our religious history! This land belongs to negroes;

other races came and crushed us because we were beautiful, strong, courageous, welcoming. We know nothing of jealousy, or bitterness or spite! These are vices that belong to the decadent white civilisation! The Lord is here with us, and for us! White men have ruined everything with their wars, their slavery, Nazism, colonisation and bizarre diseases!'

He also goaded us with claims that the Devil, in other countries, was presented as black, with a tail and pointed ears. You liked it when he said this, it made you feel rather proud, and you started to enter into a trance, like the other believers.

Mâ Lembé was overjoyed:

'Thank you, Lord! Thank you, Lord! Liwa is entering your house! Thank you for receiving him!'

After that nothing could come between you and the One True God; the time of your baptism was drawing near, and now you were speaking in tongues.

Mâ Lembé was fond of quoting tribal words of wisdom, and they come back to you now: 'The calabasse of fresh water you carried for miles on your head from the river will break on the threshold of your home.'

Two events were about to turn everything at Thanks Be to God upside down and demonstrate the wisdom of Mâ Lembé's ancestors.

Pneumatic Drill

———

YES, IT ALL COMES BACK, as if it was yesterday, down to the last detail. First there was talk in Pointe-Noire about the body of an albino girl who had been found on the Côte Sauvage. The police investigation focussed on Thanks Be to God. A vile police inspector known popularly as 'Pneumatic Drill' pursued Papa Bonheur everywhere, convinced he was the author of this hideous crime. Pneumatic Drill had questioned him ten times or more in his office at the church, which was just behind the hidden door through which he appeared at the start of each mass. Even after that he bombarded him with questions on a dozen more occasions at the PLCC, the Patrice-Lumumba Central Commissariat.

According to the inspector, Papa Bonheur had sacrificed the albino child, whom he'd taken off the streets himself two weeks earlier. Pontenegrins were shocked to learn that the young girl's body was missing several parts: head, legs and arms. The police and newspapers talked of 'ritual murder'.

Just when it seemed that the affair had gone cold for lack of clues, it re-entered the news when two highway robbers who had been imprisoned and questioned for matters unrelated to the crime imputed to Papa Bonheur threw a veritable bomb: they claimed that the pastor had offered them a hefty reward to murder the albino girl and deliver her parts to him. Specialists in such crimes argued on the radio over their significance, but they all agreed that sorcerers and certain sects used the parts of victims to cure sterility, sexual impotence, cancer, and to make lucky charms.

After the bandits' macabre confession, Pneumatic Drill renewed his attack on Thanks Be to God. He burst into the overcrowded church, interrupting mass, and took the pastor to one side and hauled him off to the police station, where Papa Bonheur denied all the brigands' allegations, swearing he was no sorcerer, that he was the leader of a church, not a sect.

He mobilised his networks in the police, received letters of support from abroad, and was cleared of all suspicion, to the great relief of the congregation.

Some of the faithful, however, continued to harbour doubts. True, he used the Bible, but some of his practices smacked of witchcraft, in particular when he instructed some of the flock to bring him back earth from a grave, or a lock of hair from a relative who had just died. In the minds of the Pontenegrins, Papa Bonheur continued to be the true culprit of the ritual murder of the albino child. It was said he must have paid a vast fortune to avoid trial and consequent imprisonment, not to say the death penalty, which was in force in our country.

Life soon enough returned to normal. The tragic fate of the albino girl was gradually forgotten. Other events took its place in the minds of the Pontenegrins: the volcano in Diosso seemed to be on the move; a pandemic of conjunctivitis shook the town; fighting was intensifying between the regime and rebel factions under the terrible Jonas Savimbi as they approached the capital Luanda to seize power.

Eight months after these various dramas, another scandal hit Thanks Be to God: rumours circulated that Papa Bonheur was the father of three children whose teenage mothers attended his church. The congregation claimed it was a plot, hatched by rival churches or by the people who had wanted Papa Bonheur's head on a platter six months earlier, at the time of the 'Albino child affair'. They resented this relentless pursuit of their pastor, and professed their continuing loyalty to him. Papa Bonheur had, as usual, denied all allegations. However, it became increasingly difficult for him to reject the evidence, given that the three mothers brought their children to every service, and the more sceptical among the faithful noted a striking resemblance between the babies and the pastor. The mothers' parents also made it known that Papa Bonheur had given them envelopes containing exorbitant sums of money, to get them either to keep silent or find a 'fake father' for their grandson.

Pneumatic Drill, dubbed 'special envoy of the Devil' by Papa Bonheur, was back again. This time, he swore, Papa Bonheur would not get away with it, not even by paying billions to his high-up friends in the police force or by brandishing letters of support from the presidents of America and Russia.

The day they handcuffed him and threw him into a police vehicle like a sack of potatoes, the faithful were surprised to see the Good Lord did not come to his aid. The pastor found himself once more on the front page of the papers, and apart from the three children he had fathered, other underage mothers began to talk, revealing that they too had had a 'thing' with Papa Bonheur, and that he had been paying their respective families maintenance for the past two years.

48

In total around fifty children were counted whose paternity was attributed by their mothers to Papa Bonheur. The trial was broadcast on the radio, and the pastor displayed a level of arrogance that annoyed even those of his own flock who were present in the courtroom. He turned the whole thing around, claiming that among his children by the various different underage mothers there was a Chosen One. This child would save the town of Pointe-Noire from decadence and the population should actually be thanking Papa Bonheur, not taking him to court and thwarting the Supreme Prophecy.

It was an indirect admission of the facts. The following day the president of the court, Judge Madzouka Ma Mbongo, summoned the mothers and their children to the hearing. He had pulled out one of the fifty children, substituting in an albino boy, whose anxious expression showed how very much he wished not to be among this group of children, none of whom he had ever met before. His parents, also albinos, had been put in a separate room from which they could watch on a screen what was happening in the courtroom. They were rather pleased to be participating in the experience and were curious to know the outcome.

Gathered together in the centre of the court, surrounded by twenty or so police officers, the children observed an icy silence that spread throughout the room. At this moment the judge asked the pastor to point out which of the children here present was the famous Chosen One.

Papa Bonheur turned around and immediately pointed to the albino whose parents were hidden in the next room. There was a great commotion in the audience, followed by a hammer blow from Judge Madzouka Ma Mbongo, calling for silence.

In a monotonous tone, the judge announced that the evidence against Papa Bonheur was overwhelming to say the least, and that he was definitely the instigator of the ritual murder of the little albino girl who had been found on the Côte Sauvage. Maître Ndokolo, widely known as the most brilliant defence lawyer in town, was unable, for all his eloquence, to save the situation. The verdict was given late in the evening: the pastor would be executed in the next few weeks. . .

These scandals, engraved in the memories of the Pontenegrins, turned you against religion once and for all. You hated it, and lost all perspective. You saw the pastor wherever you went; you even believed Papa Bonheur had not actually been executed, that his grave in Frère-Lachaise cemetery, where some of his more reckless disciples still lay flowers to this day, did not contain his body.

Were you wrong? No, in Pointe-Noire people still say the corpse of the pastor was sent to Nigeria or Ghana; that Papa Bonheur was not really from the Vili tribe, as he liked to claim; that he had no link whatsoever with the kingdom of Loango, he was a total imposter from elsewhere.

But the old folk had seen the pastor grow up; they knew his parents, could trace his family tree without skipping a single branch. Papa Bonheur was true Pontenegrin, there was no doubt about it, and from now on your shocked grandmother would simply mutter:

'What has the world come to when even those who see God act like those who never met him?'

Old Woman, Young Woman

———

DESPITE YOUR GRANDMOTHER'S OMNIPRESENCE in the longest dream of your death, and the way she welcomes the mourners at the first day of your wake while you stand watching outside your plot, you wonder why Mâ Lembé's got her back to you. She is in fact the only figure not facing you. Or who is being careful not to show you her face, even though she's the person you've spent your whole life with.

At moments you're full of doubt. Is it really her – Mâ Lembé, this woman with her back to you? Is it really her – the mother of Albertine, your dead mother? The woman who gave you the name Liwa Ekimakingaï? Who spent every minute insisting that one day you'd become a man, a respectable person, as she'd promised Albertine you would?

She looks younger here, probably somewhere in her thirties. She is tall, slender, no sign of ill health; in fact she seems dynamic, darting about at the speed of a sucking bee. There she is, preparing coffee in urns balanced on three large stones, adding wood underneath, then reviving the fire with a big fan. She seems driven by incredible energy – but is leaning on a stick. Why would a young person in good health be using a stick?

51

Your incredulity hits new depths as your 'young' grand-mother hops from place to place: her hair, dark till now, has turned grey, two fat, loosely-bound ropes falling in curls to her shoulders. She flits from youth to old age, and back again. The only link confirming it is her is the stick, since you gave it to her in the first place. It was made by old Mouboung-oulou, one of the most respected artists in Pointe-Noire. You insisted the head be made of ivory carved in the shape of a lion's head, a sign your grandmother was a woman no man could walk over. You saved up a month's salary to buy it, and Mâ Lembé only knew how much it had cost because old Mouboungoulou dropped by to compliment her on your exemplary gesture, so unlike most young people's indiffer-ence towards their parents. When he revealed the price, Mâ Lembé declared it exorbitant and preached at you for a week, threatening to sell the stick at the Grand Marché and get you a refund. She did actually put it up for sale, but no one dared touch it or ask the price. That evening she made you your favourite meal of beans and salt fish with a side of manioc leaves, and whispered:

'Thank you, little Liwa, for your gift of a third leg. I've decided not to sell the stick. Your mother, from the world beyond, opposed my decision; that's probably why no one bought it...'

Anyway, there she is, this first day of your funeral: Mâ Lembé, young or old, whichever. Her colleagues from the Grand Marché assist her, though they, paradoxically, are older. They serve coffee to all who have come. Since no one sees you're there, you move inside the plot to get a closer look at your corpse lying in its bed in the middle of the yard under a canopy of palm leaves, erected to protect you from the daytime sun. Your body is covered with white sheets, up to the neck. The tradition of Babembé people from Mouyondzi will be respected from start to finish: a corpse must remain for four days in the 'open air', with family and comforters gathered round, not in the glacial seclusion of a cupboard at the morgue, to be transported from there to its final resting place. The Babembé believe the body deserves to be treated with particular affection, since the soul remains inside it until it has turned completely to dust. This is why they talk to the corpse, to reassure and cajole, and eat beside it, telling it it's the most extraordinary corpse on earth, so beautiful, in fact, that hideous Death is ashamed to look it straight in the eye and covers itself in a cloak of darkness.

The corpses are conscious of their privileges. Some of them, indeed, can be found exploiting their position, shedding crocodile tears, getting up to tricks. Just mop their brow with a damp handkerchief, murmur a few kind words, sing a little song they knew and loved, they'll soon calm down. Then the *Mukutu* – the elderly Bembé sages whose stock of respect is proportionately linked to the number of corpses they have accompanied to their graves – declare to the marvelling throng that the deceased is now ready, that they have given a little smile acknowledging all those who have come to assist them as they cross the bar, promising not to forget them and to deliver a personal greeting in their dreams at the appropriate moment. . .

Seeing you lying here in your bed, with people all around you in the shed, no one would think you were no longer of this world. Shouts of laughter are coming now from the crowd; they're starting to settle in. People from the Trois-Cents and neighbouring parts of town are seated on mats spread out on the ground, where they'll also sleep tonight. Many of them have met before at other wakes in Pointe-Noire. They will come every evening for four days to keep vigil by your remains and every morning they will just get on with their daily business, till the day of your burial.

Your body seems at peace, but you tell yourself you've walked into a trap, believing that this first day of your funeral will never end, that it will last for a hundred years, and your happiness too will last that long. How could it not be so? Right now a day feels as long as a year, the hours last a month, the minutes a day. All this encourages you to sit back, make the most of this relaxed approach to time, enjoy the distant music that seems to restore your wings, to soar over vast gardens of white tulips, escorted by a myriad of swans with rainbow plumage. You arrive with the swans at the Côte Sauvage and the immense, sluggish silver expanse of the sea, while on the horizon a single row of whinnying white horses moves towards you, suddenly all disappearing into the belly of the ocean. As you turn back towards the empty shore, you stand for a moment, petrified: emptiness, absolute silence, a vast black hole. Perhaps because you no longer know where you are, transported by a different dream, taking you miles and miles from here. The only light you can see is the one before you – in fact, behind you – and you move forward, drawn by a vast doorway, the only way open to you. It leads to deep darkness, where, in the far distance, a weak light reveals the contours of a tiny dwelling mounted with a cross, on top of it a crow, disturbing the deep peace of the night with its insistent caw.

The Singer-Dancer-Weepers

——

YOU SEE NOW THE SECOND DAY of your funeral. Women singing, dancing and weeping all around. Yielding to their charm, you lose the habitual serenity of a corpse. It's hard not to get up off your death bed and put your arm around the waist of the prettiest one and dance with her the famous *Muntutu*, the ancestral dance of your people, the Babembé. It's also the dance of sexual initiation for young people in your tradition, imitating the gathering of a pack of boar, while within the ring of dancers, the oldest male and the most graceful female preen and tease, urged on by the whining of the rest of the pack.

These 'singer-dancer-weepers', as the Pontenegrins have come to call them, drive most of the men spread out in the chalk-drawn circle completely wild. The game is to grab the woman and hold her tight, closing your eyes as the dance gets more and more intoxicating while the mingled sweat of the woman and the man dancing shower the public, to their huge delight. Receiving the perspiration is like the ultimate reward, one that can drive a new dancer to oust the one already on the floor, as if claiming his due, while the delirious crowd urges him on.

These women all hail from the region of Bouenza. You'll hear the most risqué remarks on the curve of their backs or rather, as the Pontenegrins put it, their 'nether lands', accentuated by the way they tie a *pagne* loosely round their rear ends, leaving the belly button exposed, knowing the looks of all the men would converge there. They twist and squirm like reptiles, while their voices, some sweet, others less so, mingle till dawn with frenetic drum rolls played by muscular little men whose necks are thickly draped with cowries.

By day they dress in red from head to toe, and wave white handkerchiefs around, as though it were a wedding party. They are the talk of Pointe-Noire; the dead person is forgotten, grief is forgotten, and they know it full well. Taximen, bus conductors and other drivers who pass them at the crossroads hoot, whistle, promise to stop by and dance with them later. They laugh at this and exaggerate their suggestive moves, giving the men the full benefit of what the Pontenegrins call 'a vertiginous shake of the nether regions'. The drivers aren't kidding, they'll be there all right. Don't get the wrong wake, the women say, it's Liwa Ekimakingaï, the young commis chef, Mâ Lembé's grandson who worked at the Victory Palace hotel. That's enough information for any Pontenegrin to find it. . .

In the evening all cats are grey, and the women dress in black, smear their faces with kaolin as they sing, dance and weep with the spirits, melt into the mystery of the night and prepare your way to Mpemba, the name in Bembé legend for that arid land where the sun sets forever, where those who end up there must walk on and on forever, never turning, or be changed into pillars of salt.

The singer-dancer-weepers are not affected by their long journey. They've hopped onto Isuzu trucks in the interior, coming from different places like Kibounda, Moudzanga,

Kingouala, Kingomo, Mandou, Louboulou, Hikolo or Kimbimi, meeting at the central station in Nkayi to take a train to Pointe-Noire.

The journey lasted twenty-four hours, during which they ran through their repertoire of funeral songs, co-ordinated their dance moves, agreed once and for all who would sing soprano, mezzo-soprano or alto, and where they should stand in the plot of the deceased so that the public could hear and clearly understand the words to the songs.

There are over two hundred of them and they all stand together in the plot, their choir so well oiled that the rest of the crowd wait for them to give the note and sing the refrain three or four times over before they join in. They are paid for their ability to weep at the drop of a hat, to offer the grieving families seamless compassion and genuine tears, as though they stood before the body of their own relatives.

Mâ Lembé, who continues to appear to you with her back turned in the longest dream of your death, has not paid for their services. She could never have afforded it, and the generosity of this class of singer-dancer-weepers fills her with pride. She knows their parents, she herself has on occasion supported them, which is why all their granddaughters responded to her call today. Some have come with their mothers – it's the mothers who heard the death announcement on National Radio and asked their children to go and comfort their old friend in her grief, accompanying her grandson on his journey to the world beyond, with dancing and joy. The mothers have remained in the background, so as not to interfere with the compassionate work of their daughters, whilst offering generous helpings of veteran advice.

There is however a hidden cost to the presence of the singer-dancer-weepers: they must be fed, their travel must be paid for, since they have borrowed money in order not to miss the funeral. They are entitled to breakfast, lunch, dinner and as much coffee as they want throughout the night, to stop them nodding off . A notebook for subscriptions is passed round every day at the Grand Marché and in the streets of the Trois-Cents to cover your funeral costs. They knock at every door, and people give either a small coin or a big note; it's generally an obligation by another name – if you demur they'll quickly hurl a thinly veiled threat at you, such as:

'Not giving today? Ok, just wait till your family suffers a loss!'

The singer-dancer-weepers take turns to sleep under the stars on their mats, out in the yard, arranged around you. When one half of them falls asleep, the other half watches over you, singing, dancing, weeping, glorifying your name and lamenting your loss – worst of all would be to allow a great silence to sully your joy.

Yes, they're there, on your plot of land. This evening a large part of the rue du Joli-Soir is blocked, though no municipal authorisation has been given, to allow those Pontenegrins who wish – including those who never knew you – to lay out their mats too on the public highway. Every morning they will roll them up again.

The singing in Bembé rends the night air. The trance holds sway over the entire crowd; no one knows who's dancing with who now. Couples form, throw themselves into a wild *Muntutu* to general cheering, then vanish into a corner of the plot, replaced by couples entering the chalk circle, and drummers vigorously slap the skin of their instruments and several of the singer-dancer-weepers move away from you and start dancing, 'glued' and 'squeezed' against a stranger. They hold them right up to when they can feel their breath in their ear, then they push them away. Then they take a new partner, shaking a finger at him, while the drummers change rhythm and the beads of their sweat set off a near riot among the men, who all hope to oust the lucky dancer crushed in the arms of one of the 'friskiest' singer-dancer-weepers, the 'hottest', as the men murmur among themselves.

At this point your patience snaps, there under your awning. You gather all your strength to join in the festive atmosphere, but your limbs won't respond; you feel heavy, so heavy, the bed may well eventually collapse under your weight, terrifying all the women gathered here.

All you can do in your impotence is observe the entertainment, where everyone's having so much fun and no one wants the second night of your funeral to come to an end. You're about to shout out, make your objections known, when you notice a little way off a woman with her face smeared in kaolin. It's one of the singer-dancer-weepers, the 'friskiest', the 'hottest' of the lot, and she's ardently kissing a taxi driver, his paunch so big he can't even button his shirt. Unbuttoning her top, she guides his hand onto her breast, then the pair disappear into a car. A few minutes later you hear its engine start. . .

The Kitchen Commis

——

IT'S DAY THREE OF YOUR FUNERAL and Mâ Lembé still hasn't turned around, and your face, or rather that of your corpse, has suddenly grown darker. As though it is dawning on you that the praises offered to you through all this weeping and singing are just empty words, hollow and exaggerated. How could anyone claim you were the most beautiful corpse since the town of Pointe-Noire came into being? Deep down such flatteries merely convince you to accept what you are – dead. Life, on the other hand, will continue without you and, worse still, in ten, fifteen or twenty years, no one will remember who you were.

So it's time to start worrying about this, you think to yourself, and if you're going to react, it had better be now. You'd like to ask the flatterers to clear out now, go back to their houses; you need to lie down in your room. You've understood the tradition now, and you'd really like to go and shut yourself up in your room, as you've been longing to ever since you arrived at the plot. A dead person can only be seen twice, so you couldn't be here on your death bed under the awning *and* at Frère-Lachaise sleeping the sleep of the dead *and* hiding out in your childhood room while all these people have been expressing their sympathies to your grandmother for the last two days and nights.

Under normal circumstances, you'd be rising early, as you do every Thursday, around four thirty in the morning. No need to set an alarm; you'd be bound to hear Mâ Lembé's regular morning cough, like she's hacking her own lungs out. 'It's that tobacco she chews,' you'd say to yourself, resolving to ask her to quit, for the sake of her health. Every day she would chomp away on it, long before the first cock's crow. At the same time you'd hear her speaking, laughing out loud, as though someone was with her in the room.

One day, you remember it well, she'd yelled with rage and ordered a certain Germain to get out of her house before she called the police. The next day you asked her, acknowledging indirectly that you had seen her nocturnal visitor too:

'What was Germain doing here in the middle of the night? Is he going to keep on disturbing us like that? Because if he is, I'll deal with him myself!'

Mâ Lembé stood there, rigid with astonishment:

'So you saw him too?'

You pretended to go along with her craziness, adopting a calm, reassuring tone:

'Yes, I did, in fact I opened the door to him. I thought he'd come with good intentions...'

'That explains it. I wondered how he got in! Next time don't open the door to him, the bastard! He refused to have anything to do with your mother; he abandoned me when I was pregnant with Albertine. And another thing... I don't like his police uniform either.'

So you discovered your grandfather's name was Germain. That's all you'll ever know. His family name remains a mystery. Mâ Lembé was still haunted by this man, though perhaps he was no longer in the land of the living. In any case, she would tell you nothing more and when you got home from work at the Victory Palace that evening and tried to pick up the conversation, she was confused:

'Germain? Germain, you say? Who is this Germain? Your new boss at work?'

Other nights, it wasn't Germain but another, more peaceful presence: your mother, Albertine. These were definitely your grandmother's favourite times, when she became quite agitated, roaring with laughter, banging her stick on the ground, against the wall, her way of showing her delight. Next she's inviting your mother to pull up a stool, pouring palm wine for her, telling her the latest news of home. All they ever talked about was you and your future:

'I'm telling you, Albertine, don't worry, everything's fine, Liwa always behaves very decently. He's never missed a day's work since George Moutaka, Denise's husband, one of my colleagues at the Grand Marché, helped get him the job at the Victory Palace hotel. George is the hotel gardener, and since he's the oldest member of staff there the whites listen to him and take on anyone he recommends. In fact he has been there since the hotel opened; I think he's my age, maybe two or three years older...'

Then you heard her lower her voice:

'Yes, I know, you're going to ask if I had an affair with George Moutaka! It's true, you and I have no secrets, but it wasn't an affair. I should never have done that to my friend Denise; I just wanted to check if I could still feel a man or if my body had stopped working for good. We didn't actually 'do it', well, only once. Neither of us was really up to it – it wasn't working at his end, at mine I was too nervous and anxious because of Denise, but I wanted to help my grandson, and George did eventually find him work...'

Her voice started to tremble:

'It wasn't easy, Albertine. I didn't want to owe George anything, so I gave him a bit of money too, to put my mind at rest. I thought he would say no, but he grabbed the notes and stuffed them in his pocket without saying thank you. So far Liwa doesn't know I slept with someone and even paid them to get him a job – if he did, knowing him, he'd try to pay me back, punch the gardener in the face and resign from the Victory Palace!'

After a moment's silence she changed her tune and began showering you with compliments:

'That child is so generous, you know: when he gets his pay slip he tries to give me half! What's an old woman like me going to do with money, though? Your son, my grandson, I mean, is twenty-four now; he's been working for five years. Soon he's going to do up the house. He's already changed a few planks on the street side to spare our blushes, and he's fixed up the shower with some new metal sheets to screen it off. The worst is the roof, when it rains, but he'll see to that in a couple of months; he doesn't want me to spend a single CFA franc more. Believe me, Albertine, he isn't wasting his money, and what's more, I've never known him to bring a woman back here. But maybe he does things outside, to respect me.'

She then dissolved into tears, begging your mother to keep sending her customers at the Grand Marché, swearing she would never give the second stand to anyone else.

'You know, Albertine, that stand is what connects you and me. I've never told you this, but one day when I had nothing left, and there were almost no customers, I left my bag on your stall, with twenty thousand CFA francs inside. When I picked it up and opened it, the twenty thousand CFA francs had reproduced: now I had a hundred thousand francs! Was it you that gave me them?'

So Mâ Lembé would be coughing away at four thirty in the morning while you were getting ready for work. She'd have yelled at Germain-the-biological-father, who'd have dashed back to the land of dreams and reverted to dust, leaving your

63

grandmother to savour her last packet of chewing tobacco and maybe share a laugh and a glass of palm wine with Albertine. And as night had not yet quite vanished, you'd turn up the flame on the storm lamp. Pick up your wash bag and leave the house with a towel round your waist. You'd cross the yard and reach the shower in the corner of the plot where it overlooks the rue Albert-Moukila, on the corner with the rue du Joli-Soir. You'd tried to fix the shower up a bit, but it hasn't changed, it's just four sheets of metal bound together to make a square with a little entrance secured with a twist of wire.

You'd have two buckets of water with you that you'd filled at the other end of the plot. One bucket to soap yourself and dip the sponge in, the other to rinse off the foam before applying the towel. . .

You'd finish dressing by five in the morning and catch a bus on the avenue de l'Indépendence to the Victory Palace hotel. The bus would take you through the sleeping neighbourhood. Municipal lorries were already busy at every junction, emptying bins, flinging them onto the pavement of the thoroughfares; the noise doesn't bother the locals, they're so used to it.

It would be a long trip – the avenue de l'Indépendence goes right from one end of town to the other. You'd get a whiff of warm bread from the Cocopain bakery and see people queuing outside the Friendly Pharmacy to be sure of getting their medicines before they ran out of stock; you'd be surprised by the amount of traffic on the avenue Raymond-Paillet, mostly people on their way to work in the town centre, or returning home at the end of the day to neighbourhoods referred to by the uncharitable as 'slums'.

You'd get to the boulevard Général de Gaulle and when the bus stopped outside a restaurant called Citronelle, the rue Bouanzi, where the Victory Palace hotel is, would be only a short walk away.

Your boss, Monsieur Montoir, would be there busy giving

instructions for breakfast for the early risers, who would shortly be down from their rooms. 'Monsieur Montoir'? You preferred to call him 'Papa'. He wasn't keen at first; he felt the term aged him rather, and that at sixty-two he still had some life left in him 'around women', as he put it. But he had grown used to it, since the entire staff also called him 'Papa', and you had carefully explained to him that it was, if anything, a sign of respect, that even if he had been married to a woman of twenty everyone would have called her 'Mama', including the gardener, George Moutaka, the one who got you the job, who is now seventy-five and known to the staff as 'the Australopithecus'.

You had good reason to call Monsieur Montoir 'Papa'. It was his task to train you, and you followed him around in the kitchen like a shadow. Under his supervision you helped set up, organise supplies, peel vegetables, apples, wash the salad, prepare most of the side dishes. He needed you for the Congolese dishes, which he managed to combine with French cuisine. He had you to thank, but mostly Mâ Lembé for her ready advice. You might also be found cleaning the kitchen equipment, when you weren't helping out the pot washers. In fact you were everywhere, and your position as kitchen commis was merely what was written on your pay slip. You never planned on staying in this job all your life.

'Papa' had broached the possibility of you moving up in the profession. From kitchen commis there were at least four rungs between you and the top: cook, line cook, support and head chef. You had stopped deluding yourself: you were still exactly where you started out four years before, and the management showed no sign of moving you up. Your competence was never questioned: you were a hard worker, your motivation and sense of discipline were beyond reproach. 'Papa' himself sang your praises, commending you publicly for your admirable teamwork. The other Congolese employees laughed behind your back, and pointed out that the hotel had never had a Congolese kitchen chef and it was unlikely to happen overnight. So instead of progressing, you got your head down, focussed on your work and gained the trust of 'Papa', who at one point talked about helping you go to train at the École Ferrandi in Paris, where he had several useful connections. It was a private school, he explained, founded in the 1920s, with pupils who had gone on to have their own restaurants. And he had opened the pages of one of the Michelin Guides he kept in a corner of the kitchen to point out the names of the restaurants, the chefs, and their multiple Michelin stars.

Out of curiosity you asked:

'What about us? Have we ever had a Michelin star?'

He gave you a long, bovine stare and replied:

'Come on, there's work to be done. Peel those potatoes and make the sides. . .'

Yes, you say to yourself, this third day of your funeral: you've had enough of all this flattery; you wish they'd clear off and leave you alone with your grandmother, you need a rest, you've a long day ahead of you at the Victory Palace hotel with Monsieur Montoir. But with all this weeping and laughter who would hear your voice?

There's an ocean between these people and the longest dream of your death, a dream that is out of your grasp. You're a piece of dry wood, bobbing on the current of your illusions, with no way to escape the fourth day of your funeral, that is, your last day on earth, and by far the most important, since had you anything to say it would have to be then – after that would be too late. For good. . .

A Walk Down the Rue du Joli-Soir

———

IT'S THE FOURTH DAY, the day of your departure.

There's a smell of coffee in the air, this early morning. Some folk are still snoring on their mats. Others are washing their faces and brushing their teeth on the other side of the rue du Joli-Soir.

All of a sudden a tear trickles from your right eye. No one sees. You feel its warmth on your cheek.

A crow pops up out of nowhere, skims cross-wise over the plot, cawing as the crowd of three-day and three-night mourners looks up in fear.

Mâ Lembé no longer has her back to you. She's looking her age. She curses the fateful passerine that has just crossed back over the heads of the crowd. She shakes her stick at it and sets herself on guard, sitting there by your death bed, watching the sky as if expecting further impudence from the crow.

She swats away the flies that have come buzzing round you with a broom made of palm-leaf stalks. In her zeal to protect you from the insects, the boldest of which are heading up your nostrils, she sometimes misses her target and hits you across the face, to stifled laughter from the singer-dancer-weepers.

They've fashioned you a coffin out of ebony, with nails of plated gold. There are handles at the front, middle and back, to make it easy to lift and carry. Your photo is pasted on the sliding lid; through the glass you can see your over-made-up face, blistered cheeks, lips tightly sealed.

Joseph Mompéro, the famous carpenter from the Trois-Cents, has been most helpful: he reduced the price for making the casket by half even though it took him a whole day to make. The precision with which he sawed the planks, varnished them, put them together, then applied the final decorative touches amazed those looking on. Some of them suggested that termites, stunned by the delicacy of the work, might consider at length the options open to them, fail to reach a consensus, and decide not to attack your beautiful coffin after all.

A hearse has already been hired, and forty or so buses, not to mention the hundreds who have volunteered to drive people in their private cars. Your procession will be one of the most impressive seen in the last few years – that's what Mâ Lembé wants. As do her colleagues, who are gathered here behind the imposing figure of Sabine Bouanga. They have gone all out with the donations and exceeded the sum they were aiming for. They were involved in the logistics from the outset. Sabine Bouanga said to them all at the market:

'You only die once! This burial day has to be special! This child is our child too!'

This last day, before you leave for good, you first have to be 'walked about'. It's a long-standing tradition in the poorer districts: no one can be buried till they've been paraded through the streets.

The singer-dancer-weepers are dressed in red, for daytime. The other women are in white, the men in black, the children in orange. Sabine Bouanga and her group and the other tradeswomen sport green *pagnes* with purple head-wraps.

The crowd is immense, stretching as far as the avenue de l'Indépendence. Even though the traffic in the neighbourhood is now at a standstill, the six ripped colossi in white suits and shiny pointed black shoes manage to get through with the coffin on their shoulders. Inside it you are jolted violently as the men quicken the pace of their march to avoid the lorries heading for the Grand Marché to drop off the traders. The drivers salute the corpse with a constant honking of horns.

Kind words are spoken:

'Say hi to the folks on the other side!'

'Give our love to the ancestors!'

The crowd is striding forward now.

The procession reaches Patrice Lumumba roundabout and suddenly stops. Up front, lively discussions are taking place. Everyone is in disagreement. One side wishes to carry on, the other advises a U-turn. Meanwhile the entire town is caught in the late-morning traffic jams.

In the end they decide on a U-turn, to be on the safe side. Better not get too bogged down. If they press on straight ahead they'll reach the centre of town. They will take the avenue Moé-Kaat-Matou, which comes out where the Europeans live, the families of government ministers, as well as the city's wealthiest business men and women. In this part of Pointe-Noire the noisy atmosphere of popular funerals is strictly prohibited. There have been some memorable court cases over trouble between neighbours, and a law was passed punishing what the forces of the law referred to from then on as 'display of corpses outside private residences and in the public arena'. The movers and shakers of Pointe-Noire complained that the practice of processing with corpses littered the thoroughfares with bottles of Primus, 1664 or Ngok', not to mention banana skins, with the ruffians from the poor quarters relieving themselves against the walls of the sumptuous houses in the centre of town which were, after all, the pride of Pointe-Noire and attracted tourists to our city.

You're sulking a little in your casket. You'd have liked to have gone right through the town centre, as far as the boulevard du Général Charles de Gaulle, which you made your way along every weekday on your way to work. You would have passed the Printania and Score supermarkets, arriving at the Côte Sauvage, where you'd have recalled how, as adolescents, José, Sosthène and you would watch cormorants and hunt them with catapults. You never hurt them, you deliberately missed them; the important thing was the fun of watching them fly off clumsily, then return, landing – so short was their memory – just a few metres away. The Côte Sauvage was where you'd pick up a few fish from the Beninese fishermen, the 'Pops' as you called them, as though all Beninese were Pops, whereas in fact Pops are found only as far as Togo, and are just one of the peoples of the coastal region of south-west Benin, who brought their fishing skills with them to Pointe-Noire. You appreciated the generosity of the Pops; when they saw a young boy roaming about close to their fishing huts they'd give him a packet of sardines, mackerel or sole:

'Take that home to your parents, kids! And don't hang around too long by the water. The mermaids and other creatures of the sea could steal you away!'

This threat was enough to make you keep away from the ocean, which suddenly began growling and tossing up huge waves. On your way home you'd pass the houses of the rich whites, the bourgeois Congolese families living in the rue Félix-Eboué. The residents' cars drove by, slowing down, as though to make sure they memorised your faces, in case an offence or crime was reported. And you went back to your neighbourhood, the Trois-Cents, and the atmosphere of the Joli-Soir dance bar, with its speakers facing out into the street;

the Lebanese and Senegalese boutiques squeezed tightly together, the women selling roasted peanuts, mood balls, fried fish, the squabbles in the house plots, and cars stuck in the mud caused by the torrential rain of the previous day.

Mâ Lembé would be waiting for you at the entrance to the house; she'd take the packet of fish the Pops had given you and that day, and maybe the next day too, or the one after, you'd eat sardines, mackerel and sole...

After that no corpse had ever crossed the line to be paraded within the town centre. The police meant business; they might even impound a corpse at the police station on the Patrice Lumumba roundabout until full and final payment of a fine. Which is why the procession has turned about and you've just been taken through some of the special places of your childhood: the Tchinouka river where, again with José and Sosthène, you fished for green frogs; the Rex Quarter, where you saw your first Indian films, the karate films of Bruce Lee, westerns with Clint Eastwood and Lee Van Cleef; the Bloc-55 quarter, where you first took part in hoop races, at which you excelled; the Tata-Louboko stadium where, again with José and Sosthène, you watched matches between your district's team, FC Bisoulou Na Kwanga, and others, in particular FC Mousiki Mbila, FC Foufou Yatiya or FC Mawamba Ngouba. This last club was the arch rival of your team, having won three Ponton-la-Belle championships, while FC Bisoulou Na Kwanga had not reached a single city final in its twenty years of existence...

Mâ Lembé and her colleagues from the Grand Marché wanted you to take these marvellous images from your childhood over with you into the other world. Images of joy, laughter, dance, of the love the Pontenegrins felt towards you.

Your passing touched the whole town. It was reported in

the daily newspaper, *The Pointe-Noire Messenger*. It was widely spoken of on the radio, and young people were warned off following your example. The day after 15 August everyone was talking about you and that evening of the Independence celebrations.

In the impressive procession of vehicles accompanying you to your final resting place, many are there out of curiosity. They want to be present at the burial of 'the young man in question'. And while the procession advances along the rue du Repos, leading to the cemetery of Frère-Lachaise, they pass another, more modest procession coming away. Your procession salutes it, the other procession pays respects to yours. It's a tradition, since this road is only used by hearses or delivery vans heading for the Gabonese quarters or Mougoutsi or Nyanga.

We are approaching Frère-Lachaise and the gates stand wide open. Amidst the chanting and weeping, some tongues are loosened, claiming to possess details of the circumstances surrounding your death. Those at the back of the procession, in particular, make wild guesses. They wouldn't dare do so a few metres from Mâ Lembé, who is right at the front, behind the hearse, with Sabine Bouanga and the tradespeople from the Grand Marché, with the weeper-singer-dancers just behind her.

The people at the back of the cortege say things like:

'What a strange way to die, but he deserved it!'

'Why the hell didn't he stay at home with his grandmother that night?'

'That poor old lady, she won't last long now; she'll follow her grandson, in equally peculiar circumstances. . .'

AT FRÈRE-LACHAISE

———

Zarathustra's Promise

———

YOU OPEN YOUR EYES SUDDENLY, gasping for breath, with the feeling you almost just drowned, that while you were embarking on the longest dream of your death your body was diving into the belly of the Atlantic Ocean.

For at least a minute you wonder what you're doing here lying on top of a grave. Gradually the gentle mist overlaying everything close by starts to lift from your eyes and you remember vaguely that long before the first light of dawn you felt something like an earthquake, followed by a cyclone, that scooped you up in its fury and dropped you back down on the grave where you then fell asleep, transported by a dream in which you saw images of your childhood, adolescence and different places in Pointe-Noire, or certain key moments of your existence, people dear to you, especially Mâ Lembé and Albertine, the two loves of your life, one who stayed close till your final hour, the other you never knew. . .

Just for now there's nothing here you recognise.

The one reassuring thing is your clothing, which hasn't

changed for five days: orange crepe jacket with wide lapels that you've folded down, green fluorescent shirt with a broad, three-button collar and round musketeer cuffs; white bow tie, which you quickly straighten, thinking of Mâ Lembé, who hated when you let it slip to one side. And looking further down, the purple flared trousers are pretty unmissable, as are your red lacquer Salamander shoes with white laces, tossed casually around the grave.

It's starting to sink in now: you're at Frère-Lachaise, and this is your new home. . .

You visited Frère-Lachaise before, for the committal of your maternal uncle, Jean-Pierre Mouberi. He was actually an old acquaintance of Mâ Lembé who sometimes came round to the rue du Joli-Soir, though the nature of his relationship with your grandmother was never clear to you, apart from the fact that he too came from the Bouenza region. As soon as he turned up, usually at a weekend, your grandmother would send you to buy 1664 beers at the Joli-Soir, and a litre of red, then you'd disappear for the best part of half a day, leaving them to sort out 'family matters', to quote Mâ Lembé. By the time you got home, the man was ready to leave, smiling from ear to ear, sometimes with a tail of his shirt trailing, or part of his collar hidden under the lapel of his short-sleeved jacket.

Forestalling the questions trotting round in your mind, Mâ Lembé would say, without believing it herself:

'Jean-Pierre Mouberi's your uncle. . .'

Then she would add, as though to put an end to discussion:

'That's right, he's your uncle, let's put it that way, don't go asking yourself a thousand questions.'

And so you always considered him your uncle. Before starting up his scooter he would take out a wad of notes and hand them to your grandmother:

'That's for little Liwa.'

The Vespa would spring into life, and Mâ Lembé would go to the entrance to the plot to watch his motorcycle pass the Joli-Soir and vanish over the horizon, swallowed up by the traffic on the avenue de l'Indépendence.

'What a good man Jean-Pierre is,' she'd murmur, not realising you were just behind her. . .

Jean-Pierre Mouberi was killed in a traffic accident over by the Rex cinema. One of the lorries that deliver the projection reels to the city cinemas hit him as he was coming out of his mother's house on the rue Louboulou and turning left to go home. His mind was probably on the conversation with his mother, whose health was declining, and he hadn't had the presence of mind, or the instinct, to give way to the vehicle hurtling towards him from the right. . . Everyone in Pointe-Noire knew this intersection was one of the most dangerous in the city. People had lost count of the number of accidents, most of which were fatal. The inhabitants of the Rex district had petitioned the municipality unsuccessfully for lights to be placed at the junction. Every time there was an accident the mayor was quick to promise the lights were coming:

'It will take time for the lights to arrive – they have to come from France, and the French have their own traffic problems.'

In the end the population came up with an explanation for why the mayor wouldn't install lights to make the traffic safer at the junction of the two thoroughfares. He needed the accident victims, especially the dead ones, in order to get re-elected: his sorcerers were the greediest in the whole country, they wanted payment in souls. So the more people died, the longer the mayor stayed in power. Those who didn't support this thesis, which was popular in the Rex district, tended to blame outsiders, the little West African tradespeople who competed ruthlessly with each other at the junction, selling waxed *pagnes*, scrap metal, essential items and sweet treats for children. Many people thought that the reason traders did better here than at the Grand Marché was because they bought back the souls of dead people like your uncle Jean-Pierre Mouberi and gave them board and lodging at the back of their shops.

At the time of the accident Mâ Lembé insisted you pay your last respects to the 'relative' who paid for most of your school supplies each September:

'A nephew must attend the burial of his uncle, to receive his blessing for a long life. Besides, you won't have to spend all those hours studying your lessons now; he'll whisper the answers to you from up above, you can just copy them down, you'll get top grades. . .'

You remember a cemetery with white painted walls. No weeds grew between the graves, the avenues were straight, meeting at the crossroads opposite you now, with a huge fountain where myriads of birds with colourful plumage came to quench their thirst. Several famous people were buried at Frère-Lachaise, including the national poet, Jean-Baptiste Tati-Loutard, and Jean Félix-Tchicaya, the politician. The former was known for his poem 'Baobab', which you recited at school, and from which a few lines had been taken for his epitaph.

> O Baobab, when I am sunk in gloom
> And can't recall the tune of any song
> Then stir the throats of all your birds for me
> And let their song encourage me to live
> And when the ground gives way beneath my feet
> Let me scrape up the earth around your roots:
> May it then gently come to cover me!

As for the deceased politician Jean Félix-Tchicaya, you learned – though only later, while studying for your general certificate of secondary education – that he had been the first Congolese representative at the Assemblée nationale in Paris in the 1940s, back when the Congo was a French colony. All schoolchildren learn by rote – without understanding what it means – that it was Félix-Tchicaya who first asked for Pointe-Noire to become a proper commune...

Alas, the time when the dead at Frère-Lachaise rested in peace with no class distinctions was now long gone. The rich had begun to protest at what they called 'laxness'. They drew up a public petition and published it on the front page of *Mweti*, the country's main newspaper, sickened by the idea that their honourable dead might lie cheek by jowl with bums from the poor districts who couldn't lie quietly in their coffins. The rich maintained they'd been betrayed by politicians, since the promise made by the Head of State, President Mokonzi Ayé alias Zarathustra, to create a replica of Père-Lachaise in France here in Pointe-Noire had been shelved. Now the rich had supported Papa Mokonzi Ayé alias Zarathustra by supplying him with the arms needed for the coup d'état which had put him in power for an indefinite period. These same supporters also went on to back Papa Mokonzi Ayé alias Zarathustra's decision to modify the Constitution so there would be no elections in his lifetime. And in case anyone should be waiting for his death to declare their candidacy for his succession, a small clause in the new law stated that his son would automatically assume power the day his father died.

According to Pointe-Noire's capitalists, not just any old white in France got to be buried at Père-Lachaise, the most famous cemetery in the world. The rich Congolese invoked the historic and prestigious nature of the French burial ground, which took its name from François d'Aix de La Chaise, Louis XIV's – the Sun King's – confessor, whom Papa Mokonzi Ayé alias Zarathustra admired – even as far as dreaming of a seventy-two-year reign like the French monarch's.

They would moan:

'What's the point of being rich in this life if you end up in a grave next to the idle poor? The French know what's what: it's easier to get a chair in literature or pass the exam for the National Business School than to secure a little plot in Père-Lachaise!'

In conclusion – and to silence any remaining sceptics – they said that people visited the cemetery in Paris as they would a museum, with its famous inhabitants from all over the world: the singer Édith Piaf, or the writer Molière, whom you'd studied at school.

In the same year that Papa Mokonzi Ayé alias Zarathustra promised a replica of Père-Lachaise to the well-to-do, the little people jumped the gun by dubbing what had always been modestly called the 'Cemetery of the Poor', despite also welcoming the rich, 'Frère-Lachaise'. In actual fact, the term 'poor' in the old name meant 'deceased', rather than 'impoverished'. Caught on the hop, and in an attempt to avert the rising discontent of the middle-class citizens, and the possible threat to the regime, Papa Mokonzi Ayé alias Zarathustra declared the creation of a cemetery called 'Cemetery of the Rich', after the advisors to the Head of State persuaded him not to listen to those who suggested names like 'Père-Lachaise of the Congo' or 'Père-Lachaise of Pointe-Noire'. The danger would be to let the people think that the government had been inspired by the Frère-Lachaise, which was becoming ever more popular in the country, and not by the famous French cemetery in the rue du Repos, in the twentieth arrondissement of Paris. The Pontenegrins, known to be an unruly lot, refused henceforth to acknowledge that the tarmacked road to the cemetery of the poor was called the rue Papa-Mokonzi-Ayé. They referred to it by the name of the French street leading to Père-Lachaise, the rue du Repos, even though the government had not recognised the name, and it was formally forbidden to use it on maps of the town.

Once the name 'Cemetery of the Rich' had been selected by presidential decree, the national army were tasked with digging up the famous people in Frère-Lachaise and moving them to the new patch, where the tombs are proper little houses, attracting tourists from all over the world.

Even if we had managed to raise the necessary sum, thanks to the subscriptions of the Trois-Cents district and the women of the Grand Marché, Mâ Lembé's request to bury you at the Cemetery of the Rich, purely for the prestige, would have been smartly turned down by the city authorities. The refusal would not have been connected to your social standing, since people of modest means had been known to be laid to rest here, if their family had taken out a bank loan repayable over a ten-year period. Apart from the requirement for the deceased to have been morally irreproachable to gain a place at the Cemetery of the Rich you had to be someone who is 'well dead'. Now you were 'badly dead', a view still held by the people of Pointe-Noire, in spite of the big parade they gave you, bringing you here. Yes, the circumstances leading to your death created a real outcry in the Cemetery of the Rich. . .

The DHR

———

YOU MOVE SEVERAL METRES AWAY from what you now think of as *your* mango tree, which identifies the position of your grave. Now that the sun seems to be burning the weeds growing round some of the tombs, the tree is your only source of shade. You're careful not to walk on the other gravestones. Some are kept nice and tidy, as if they were homes occupied by living people, others look like they've been deserted, with no clue left as to the identity of their occupant.

You look around at the various different epitaphs, some carved onto a tomb, others on a headstone in letters picked out in gold or silver. Some inscriptions are lengthy and over-blown, others laconic and brief, as though the departure of the relative had come as a welcome relief.

Two of the inscriptions almost knock you sideways. How could such flagrant errors, handicaps which should have dis-suaded any self-respecting corpse from passing over to the other world, have slipped through?

On one of the tombs was written in capital letters:

TO OUR DEAR SISTER, MAY HER SOUP REST IN PEACE

Was it her soul resting in peace, or her soup, you wonder, disingenuously. Unless, since you are seeing things muddled – the only outstanding anomaly from this morning – 'p's now replace 'l's, and vice versa. Which raises questions about the consonants in the rest of the inscription. Was she 'dear' or 'dead' or 'deaf'? In the end you decide to give the family of the dear soul/soup the benefit of the doubt.

Two tombs further on – and this is the one that really grabs your attention, since of all the epitaphs you have read up till now this is the one you find most ambiguous and humiliating – you read:

PROSPER MILANDOU DIRECTOR OF HUMAN
RESOURCES LIES FOREVER IN OUR HEARTS

Did the family members of this person think the deceased was actually lying about being dead? You loved writing and spelling at school, and now you start mentally quibbling, thinking 'lying' could either mean 'deceiving' or 'laid to rest'.

Longing to clarify the epitaph, you pick a piece of charcoal up off the ground. It won't be that difficult: the cross is white, you just need to cross out 'lies" and insert 'here lies' at the start of the inscription. You mutter the correct formulation to yourself: 'Here lies Prosper Milandou Director of Human Resources, forever in our hearts.'

Just as you are about to add 'Here lies' you hear a footstep behind you and someone bellows:

'I'm right behind you! I mean, I'm right in front of you!'

You still can't see anyone.

'If you want to see me, look the other way – you should be used to it by now! I'll put you out of your misery or you'll end up in the bottomless pit yourself. I noticed your head was actually already pointing towards the black hole. . .'

He comes up to you and sniffs your clothes:

'Wow, you sure smell of Mananas! Did they spray on too

much at the morgue or what? And what's this ridiculous clown suit you're wearing? Anyone would think you'd died on stage! And this fluorescent green shirt! I didn't know round musketeer cuffs were still in fashion! Ok, ok, I'll stop. Clothes don't make the man, as they say, even if we recognise him by them. Let's talk about something serious.'

He palpates your calves, then your thighs. Embarrassed by this approach from someone you don't actually know, you proffer your hand in an attempt to remind him of the basic rules of courtesy.

He looks at it for a moment, refuses to shake it, and looks away:

'No need for fancy manners round here. Try spinning round till you drop to the ground. . .'

You don't react. The man insists:

'If you want to see things around you the right way up you'd better do as I say.'

'Why should I believe you?'

'Because we've all been in your shoes! Or I could leave you as I found you. . .'

You comply this time, not asking yourself why he might help you, what could be in it for him. You step away from the edge of the grave, spin round giddily on the spot several times, as though performing some diabolical dance with an imaginary partner, staggering under your own momentum, with the feeling that everything's falling down on top of you, the clouds down below are rising towards you, while at your feet objects are leaving the ground and floating at chest level, then lingering in the air while you fall to the ground, gasping for breath. . .

You feel a hand grasp your shoulder, pulling you up. When your eyes are still half closed you get two violent slaps on each cheek.

'Hey, what are you hitting me like that for?'

'To stop you feeling dizzy!'

'I should like to point out to you that—'

'Oh, leave the formalities to the living, we're all friends here...'

The slaps certainly shook you up; your interlocutor seems more real now, and the sky is up above, the ground below.

He is pleased with this outcome.

'Better now?'

He is dressed in a grey suit with a black, badly tied cravat, but you resist adjusting it for him, though it's always tempting; it goes back to your childhood, when Mâ Lembé used to struggle with your bow tie before you set off to church at Thanks Be to God.

He's a tall guy, limp hair drawn back off his face and tied in a ponytail, a greying beard of such volume that his mouth is completely hidden when he speaks. He must be over seventy. In his hands is a plastic bag, in which you can see bananas and mandarins.

He looks at your feet:

'Did they really bury you in your bare feet?'

You nod across to where your shoes are tossed.

'Don't lose them. Go get them quick, put them back on. Our shoes are what remind us of the vastness of the world. The living always bring us flowers, never shoes. They spend their whole lives putting shoes on, but it doesn't occur to them that the road of death is a long one too, and we'd like some shoes to walk in! We're a long time dead.'

He adjusts his tie which the rising wind has blown to one side:

'I wasn't here when you arrived, I do apologise; I can't be everywhere at once. I spent the national holiday at the rich folk's cemetery; I stayed on for a few days, and a friend mentioned to me while we were enjoying a few glasses of Pinot noir that there was a newbie on my patch. I was annoyed because this area is already bursting at the seams, but they keep on sending us new occupants and when we complain to

Black Mamba they take no notice. How will it all end? Trampling each other underfoot, like in some communal grave? There's a bit of space over by the wall there, no one wants to live there; they say the wall gives the dead nightmares. Nonsense, of course!'

He takes a piece of fruit from his plastic bag:

'I know you've got a mango tree here, would you like a mandarin for a change?'

'No thanks, I'm not hungry.'

He brings out another piece of fruit:

'Would you prefer a banana?'

'No, I'm really not hungry.'

'No worries, my friend, it's like that to start with, but you'll get hungry in the end. If you want to live here you have to feed yourself. You'll be all right now I've sorted out your sense of direction and perception...'

He peels the banana:

'Mm, delicious! Sure you won't have some?'

'No...'

'Your loss... It's pathetic, people who die and don't know what to do next.'

He glances over at your tomb:

'They haven't written anything on it! Not even an epitaph riddled with errors, like mine? What's your name?'

'Liwa Ekimakingaï...'

'You don't say! Quite a mouthful! Fancy being called "Death was afraid of me" and ending up here! Don't you have a European first name, like most Congolese?'

'No...'

'So you're from Congo-Zaïre, where they don't have Christian names! I might have known!'

'No, I'm from Congo-Brazzaville, and my name's the one given to me by my grandmother.'

'Well, I shall simply call you Liwa, Congo-Zaïre or not!'

He nods at the grave a couple of metres behind you:

'So what were you doing to that grave with your bit of charcoal?'

'I just wanted to correct the mistake; it's disrespectful to Prosper Milandou...'

'That's not your job! Do you know Prosper Milandou?'

'No, but if I was him I wouldn't have accepted that inscription!'

He stifles a laugh:

'Well, you and Prosper Milandou are about to meet!'

'Really? Where?'

'Right here, right now. He's talking right at you...'

You are petrified. You try to think how you can take back what you've just said about his epitaph.

Too late. He grabs the piece of charcoal from your hands, hurls it a few metres off and turns to you with his face set hard, thundering:

'Quit that silly game round here! I'm old enough to be your grandfather, if not your great-grandfather! You haven't come here to correct mistakes!'

He's been holding on to the banana peel. Now he throws it behind him.

'Let me tell you this: in Frère-Lachaise there are school masters, teachers of French, Greek and Latin, people with degrees and doctors of this, that and the next thing, people with such super-brains you wonder how come they're dead and not still with the living, sharing their super-intelligence! "Mistakes" never stopped them coming to live here! They're humble, not all puffed up like you! Who do you think you are? Besides, do the dead write the epitaphs? It's the living that get it wrong, not us! Think you're better than me at writing, do you? You think if we do Mérimée's dictation you'll score higher than me?'

He looks over at the grave.

'So my tombstone is riddled with errors, is it? And? Where's *your* epitaph then?'

You turn around and start walking over to your grave.

You hear him come running up behind you:

'Wait! Please wait, I'm sorry I got worked up about nothing, I still have some things to say to you. . .'

You sit down under your mango tree. Prosper Milandou sits down too, facing you, like a shadow, but with a slight distance between you.

His manner is serious now; he's no longer the excitable person he was a few minutes ago:

'By rights I shouldn't be here; I should be at the Cemetery of the Rich. They do ask me over from time to time,' he murmurs, looking up at the sky, his face growing steadily darker.

You're leaning back comfortably against the trunk of your mango tree, almost nodding off; you hear his voice in the background, as he launches into a long, well-oiled soliloquy without the slightest hesitation, proof that he has told his story thousands of times over to new arrivals in this place. Why risk interrupting him?

'Prosper Milandou's the name, son of the great attorney Zacharie Milandou. I was a big shot back in France. . .'

He observes the effect of his words on you and, seeing you open your eyes, accelerates:

'Back then – I can't put an exact date on it, so much dust has settled on it since, and when I tell my sorry tale to beginners like you they think I'm a braggart, just bigging myself up! Believe me, Liwa, in France I held the post of Director of Human Resources in a large company, the Lyon Water Board. . . .They called me DHR, as you saw on my epitaph, though you were only interested in the mistakes. As Director of Human Resources I had a huge office to myself on the tenth floor of a modern building in the seventh arrondissement, near the Champ de Mars. My office had a view of the Eiffel

Tower, and I would stand proudly at the vast bay window and watch tourists from all over the world flock to visit the monument.

'Was there any finer situation for an office in the whole of Paris? There was not! I needed to show myself worthy of the privilege. So I would dress in a grey suit with black tie, as you see me now, polished shoes, centre parting. I carried a black leather attaché case, heavy with files which I started working through as I drove round in my company car. My chauffeur, a Cameroonian who was also my hairdresser, would hurry round to open my door, saying, as I stepped out: "Have a good day at work, Monsieur le Directeur." Entering the lobby of our company's building, where people also wished me a deferential "good morning", I would bow my head and give a little smile before pressing the button for the lift to take me to the tenth floor. I then walked down a very long corridor, greeting my colleagues as I passed, stopping for a few minutes at reception to look down my list of meetings, before entering my office for discussions with my secretaries, two French women I had recruited fresh from their diplomas in Public Relations. I basically chose them because they had been at Paris Dauphine University in the sixteenth arrondissement, where I myself had studied twenty years earlier. At least, that's the answer I gave anyone who accused me of not having – as they put it – "given black women a chance", and hiring white women instead.

'I was one of the most respected people in my field. As they entered my office, people felt intimidated – perhaps by the red carpet covering the one hundred and fifty square metre space assigned to me alone. The walls were painted sky blue, tempering the seriousness of my work. It's not easy, recruiting the right people to the right job, as well as having to break the news to family men and women that they were no longer part of the business and were currently the object of a process of dismissal. A Director of Human Resources is never popular. On the one hand people reproach them for not hiring such and such a candidate, though they were the best; on the other people hold a grudge against them for firing so and so, though he had a family to feed, funeral costs to meet, a mortgage to repay, that kind of thing. They're seen as a cold monster, a remorseless killer, a sharp-toothed chainsaw, the man – or woman – from whom all injustice flows. That's probably why they need an enormous office, so someone coming in for a job interview or being made redundant doesn't feel hemmed in, caught in a trap. It's easier when you're giving good news, such as: "Your application has caught our interest, we've decided to make you a job offer." But it is painful to make solemn announcements such as: "As indicated in our preliminary interview of twelfth March last, we have decided to terminate your employment."

'I hope it is by now clear that this is the job I did for over twenty years, and which I held in Paris as recently as last year, when, on Christmas Eve, I decided to quit my position in France and accept an offer from the Congo National Electricity Company, here in Pointe-Noire. Little did I know that my life was about to take a new direction. . .

'Liwa, are you still listening to me?'

You nod. He lifts his head to the sky, as though his story were written somewhere in the clouds, and he needed to check it before continuing:

'Some of my compatriots used to say I was one of the few Africans who hired and fired whites on their own continent! I am not being unduly modest when I say it was absurd of them to reduce my role to a mere question of one colour finding favour over another. I didn't care in my professional life if people were white, black, yellow or any colour of the rainbow. I had studied employment law in order to become as competent as possible in everything I did and to disregard the social status of the individual. I was lucky enough to start out very young, younger than you, straight from my degree at Paris Dauphine University, where I came top of my year and immediately joined the Human Resources department of the Lyon Water Board. My ability to motivate my colleagues took me to the rank of assistant to the director, and when the latter was poached by the competition I was appointed in his place. After two decades at the firm I really felt like part of a family. I got whatever I wanted, including my office, which I personally asked to have extended, insisting, too, on the choice of furniture. I had a round wooden table in the centre of the room for meetings with my team. The walls were decorated with paintings I had bought all over the world in the course of my professional travels. On a long wooden dresser I arranged statuettes, mostly from Central Africa. On the same piece of furniture I also placed shells and my collection of exotic insects from Madagascar and the Comoros. I usually worked either on the sofa or at the round table, from where I had a better view of the Eiffel Tower and of the planes crossing the Parisian skyline. I should also make clear that on my office shelves were not only books connected to my profession but also the great classics of literature: Charles Dickens, Mark Twain, John Steinbeck, Ernest Hemingway, Chinua Achebe, Alexandre Dumas, Camara Laye, Fernando Pessoa, as well as Dostoyevsky and Dino Buzzati. These illustrious writers kept silent company with me, watched me while I worked, received visitors, held discussions with my colleagues, who were also deeply impressed to find that I was not uniquely attracted to works connected with my own professional interests.'

He checks again you're not asleep, which you're not, and is encouraged by your constant, unwavering interest:

'Yes, I might have been content with this extraordinary

professional success had I not received a visit from Rodolphe Xavier Kalala, Finance Minister of the Congo, last December tenth. I remember the date, because I had until Christmas Day to make a decision. Rodolphe Xavier Kalala burst into my office. Although he had not made an appointment, I agreed to see him, along with his advisors – a member of my country's government didn't turn up at my place of work every day. He walked round and round my office, admiring my works of art, leafing through a few of the books on my shelves before coming to the matter in hand:

"'I expect you are wondering about the reason for my visit, dear Prosper Milandou…'"

"'Far be it from me, Minister, though I must confess I am surprised to receive such an honour…'"

"'Well then, I'll come straight to the point…'"

'He paused for breath for a moment, then continued:

"'Your experience will be very useful to us in developing our National Electricity Company… Better still, we need to make ethnic appointments in the country's top jobs if we are to regain power again one day. The northerners, by which I mean the Mbochi, seized it from us and effectively sidelined all managers from the south, I was going to say from the Pool region, especially those of us from the Kongo. Surely a Kongo like yourself should play a part in the recovery of our dignity…?'"

'Before taking his leave, the minister handed me his card and said, while shaking me warmly by the hand:

"'Have a good think about my proposal, dear Prosper Milandou, and call me if you decide that you genuinely love your own country and have had enough of working for a different one…'"

'I telephoned my mother, who was very keen for me to return to Pointe-Noire. My younger sister less so:

"'Why would you come back to the Congo when you can boss whites around in France? Please don't come back here!

The northerners have already killed Papa, and now they'll try to involve you in their political intrigues. I don't want that to happen, brother – you must stay there with the whites! Haven't you heard – Minister Rodolphe Xavier Kalala is a southerner who's sold out and does deals with the northerners to get rid of our managers who could run the country?"

'My sister Georgette was not wrong. We were still small children at the time of our father Zacharie Milandou's death. We lived between France and the Congo – Papa was a lawyer at the Paris Bar. The government had asked him to become Minister of Justice in our country. But he knew it was a strategy designed to sow division between him and his university fellows, Maître Jacques Mbemba, Maître Bouzoba Yayi and Maître Makayabou Yakoubola, with whom they had set up the Congolese Human Rights Committee to denounce, from France, political crimes perpetrated by the ruling regime. They were supported by well-established French lawyers, led by that luminary of the Bar, Jacques Vergès.

'Papa declined the offer of a portfolio at the Attorney General's office. Two weeks later one of the members of the Congolese Human Rights Committee accepted it: Maître Bouzoba Yayi, who is believed by all the Congolese, to this day, to have been responsible for poisoning our father in a Congolese restaurant in the Château Rouge quarter, in the eighteenth arrondissement of Paris. . . Our father died without our ever knowing exactly why. The government wanted to repatriate his body quickly, to pay him a national tribute, but our mother opposed them: Papa had always wanted to be buried in France. At the Pantin cemetery, where many of his fellow activists were buried. So that is where he lies and every year without fail on All Saints' Day, when I was in France, I would lay flowers on his grave, and if I wasn't in Europe I would get some delivered. . .

'So you see, Liwa, I found myself on the horns of a Cornelian dilemma. Should I come back and work in the Congo, or stay in my comfortable situation in France? Despite Georgette's opposition, I phoned Minister Rodolphe Xavier Kalala, as I'd stopped sleeping and could think of nothing but his proposal. And I had the feeling that my father would have agreed with me. The day before I had gone to Pantin cemetery to explain things to him, and got the impression, from a bird that kept flying around close by, that he was giving me his approval...

'After just half an hour's conversation with Rodolphe Xavier Kalala, I officially agreed, and said I would resign from the Lyon Water Board, offering my services to the Congo National Electricity Company.

'The Lyon Water Board tried to hold on to me, but I was really warming to the idea of being useful to my country-men and women, and perhaps also of doing better than my father, and helping our own ethnic group. Two months later I was finally free to go, leaving everything behind me. It wasn't exactly difficult, being forty-five, unmarried and childless, but it was the life I had chosen and it would take too long to explain it here...'

For the first time you interrupt him:

'So you never had any children?'

He shows no surprise at the question, pleased, still, to have your attention.

'No, Liwa, we wanted to adopt but we gave up; the waiting list for certification by the child support services was too long. We knew what was going on, though; our profile as a couple didn't match what they were looking for.'

'Because you were black?'

'No, not at all – we were what they call a mixed couple.'

'But if your wife was white why did they turn you down?'

'No, my other half was a man...'

'...?'

'Yes, you heard me right.'

'So you're. . .'

'I'm a homo? Is that what you're calling me, like the rest of them?'

'No, no, but just looking at you, I wouldn't say. . .'

He bursts out laughing.

'My boyfriend was a beautiful man, brilliant and generous. I met him on holiday at Noirmoutier and at first he was prepared to come and live with me in Pointe-Noire, but he changed his mind once I settled back in the Congo: he got together with one of our best friends, a guy I'd hired at the Lyon Water Board. Such is life. . .'

'You still seem upset about it, sir. . .'

'Liwa, why don't you just call me by name. . .?'

'It's really hard. . .'

'Well, there's all the time in the world here, you'll get used to it. . . Anyway, where was I? Oh yes, so I got back to the Congo just one week before they announced some terrible news on Congolese National Radio: Minister Rodolphe Xavier Kalala had been found dead after suffering a stroke. His post remained vacant for over a month, while there I was with no job. I was living at the Meridian Hotel in Brazzaville waiting for the ministerial decree for my new position to be signed by the new minister, Joachim Okabando. A seventy-year-old northerner of the same ethnic group as the President of the Republic, often acting as his fall guy. Broadly speaking, Joachim Okabando was said to do the dirty work necessary to keep the regime in power. He was thought to be responsible for a number of political assassinations, to have got away with it thanks to the frequent intervention of the president, and later on he would often pop up at the head of such and such a public service or in charge of one of the big national companies. Joachim Okabando's disdainful manner riled me, the few times I talked to him on the phone. He acted like I was bothering him, fixed appointments with me which he cancelled at the last minute. All this time I was paying my

95

hotel bills myself, as well as the cost of my mother and sister's many trips from Pointe-Noire to see me. When my appointment was finally signed off, without my being received by the new minister, even though I was in Brazzaville and his ministry was less than five hundred metres from my hotel, I took a plane one Sunday afternoon, landing in Pointe-Noire one hour later. An official residence – extremely modest – awaited me in the city centre. The house was situated on the third floor, with a view of the morgue of the Adolphe-Cissé hospital, from which I could not help watching families leaving in tears, bodies being carried on stretchers like animals. All that remained was for me to visit my place of work, meet the people I was to work with, and above all move into the office that had been assigned to me as the new DHR of the Congo National Electricity Company...'

For a moment he savours the continuing impact of his tale on me, then goes on:

'When I saw the offices of the management of the Congolese company I almost passed out. The now deceased minister, Rodolphe Xavier Kalala, had sworn to me in Paris that I would be so pleased with my office I would spend more time at work than in my official residence. At the start, as I glanced around what everyone proudly called the "open plan" office, I told myself this was probably for the whole of my team, and that my personal office was perhaps elsewhere. But the head of logistics told me that I would be working there too, among all the others on the payroll, because the new minister, Joachim Okabando, was seeking to reduce inequality between management and other employees in state businesses. Joachim Okabando, who had done a brief internship in the United States, wanted to achieve what he had seen in other offices, where people talked to each other without protocol, working together without partitions or walls to keep them apart. It was a new way of doing things, which was apparently working out well in a number of Congolese public companies.

'Up to that point I had only ever worked in a private space, so this work place felt to me like a great barn or warehouse, where people came and went, talking loudly, laughing loudly, not concentrating on their work. Tables were pushed up next to each other, files lay all around in untidy piles next to old computers, to which people had stuck Post-it notes with their names on. How could my so-called collaborators work naturally if they felt I was constantly keeping my eye on them?

'These were new offices and I learned after three months that before then the premises of the National Electricity Company had been in a high tower near the Victory Palace hotel. Joachim Okabando had set up the headquarters of his private businesses there, and each boss had their own office, with no one working in an open plan. . .

'One morning I woke up feeling really angry. I called my team together and suggested we write a letter to Minister Joachim Okabando, asking him to give us back the premises in the tower by the Victory Palace hotel, while the members of the ministerial cabinet could come and work in our open space.

'I said quite loudly:

'"This is a democratic decision. Those in favour of sending this petition to the minister raise their right hands. . ."

'There was a silence. I repeated my request, but no one raised their hand and everyone lowered their gaze. Just as I was thinking that everyone was opposed to my decision I saw a hand go up at the back of the room. It belonged to a young woman I suddenly recognised. It was Pauline Moukila-Massengo, the woman in charge of maintenance for our office and for the whole of the rest of the building. I looked at her for a few seconds then said:

'"Madame Moukila-Massengo, I admire your courage as much as I am disappointed by the cowardice of my colleagues. But I'm sorry, I won't be writing this letter and we will continue to work in our present conditions, since that seems to be what everyone wants. . ."

'Over the next few days I made enquiries about Pauline Moukila-Massengo. I consulted her folder in the personnel file. I discovered that she had a baccalaureate in commercial management and was a single mother to two children, aged four and six. Their father had been sentenced for desertion of the marital home and had paid no alimony for years. He had also been found guilty in court of repeated conjugal violence and was forbidden to approach Pauline Moukila-Massengo's house.

'I was very sad to learn all this, and all night long I tried to think of ways of setting her back on her feet, of giving renewed meaning to her existence. She mustn't spend her life cleaning for the National Electricity Company, I wouldn't be comfortable with that. So I summoned her to my office and that day she had the surprise of her life:

'"Madame Moukila-Massengo, I have decided to send you to Paris for six months, to the Lyon Water Board, to train in personnel management. All expenses will be covered by our company, including your childcare in France. I need you. When you get back, you will be my deputy."

'As she was leaving my office, with tears in her eyes, I said to myself that I had definitely just made the most important appointment of my entire career. At least, that was what I believed. I had no idea, at that point, that things would take a quite different turn, and that this decision would deeply affect the course of my own life. . .'

Prosper Milandou rummages again in his plastic bag and brings out another piece of fruit.

'Telling you all that has really made my stomach rumble...
Sure you don't want a mandarin?'

'No, thank you, I'm still not hungry...'

'A banana then?'

'No, thank you.'

He peels a banana and repeats the words you have already heard:

'It's pathetic to see people who die and don't know what to do next.'

He makes a hole in the ground, buries the banana skin, covers it and continues with his tale:

'Five months after Pauline Moukila-Massengo's departure for France, a man turned up at the entrance of the National Electricity Company. Around sixty. His lips were reddened, most likely from alcohol. He asked to meet me, he wanted to give me something. He was carrying a large shoulder bag. They let him in, told him where to find me: in the middle of the *open space*. The man walked purposefully towards me, and when he was within two metres of me, took his bag from his back, placed it on the ground and opened it. I heard my colleagues start screaming as they made for the door and the emergency exits like rats in a forest fire. The man was pointing a shotgun at me, yelling:

'"My wife was your mistress! Pauline was your mistress! Sick of being a paedo, were you? Think I didn't know about it? You sent her to France to hide it!"

'I never heard the shot. They say if you hear it, you're not dead. I put my hand to my chest, from which a warm liquid flowed. A direct hit to my heart. After that, total darkness, till the day I felt what you must have felt too, the day after your burial. That is to say, today at first light. Yes, I felt a jolt that opened up the earth around me, and I was sucked up by what felt like a cyclone, and found myself on a hillock with a cross on top; to be precise, on top of the grave where you were trying to correct my sister's mistake in the epitaph, which she probably made in a state of distress at losing me. I could have corrected it but why destroy such a poignant souvenir? At any rate, I was glad I was breathing. It was a victory for me; it meant I was entering another life. Of course I felt a burning temptation to return to the land of the living, to go and attack the man who had shot me dead in broad daylight, surrounded by my colleagues. I resisted it – people here advised against it. They told me things had always turned out badly for anyone wishing to return to the land of the living in search of revenge. No one could recall a resident of Frère-Lachaise who had managed it, and the few who had gone back and returned to their grave had gone to do good, to relieve the terrible sadness of people suffering from the loss of their loved one. But how many really want to venture back to the land of the living for such a good cause? I had good reason to fight back at Minister Joachim Okabando and even at my replacement, who was in fact his cousin. Even worse, it was rumoured throughout Pointe-Noire that Joachim Okabando had ordered my assassination in order to free up a job for his cousin. My killer really was the father of Pauline Moukila-Massengo's children, a tramp from the Côte Sauvage who had been given a bundle of notes, told I was seeing the mother of his children, that I intended to change their names to Milandou. . . I didn't really care, actually, I didn't want to get mixed up in all that again. After a while folks here started to trust me and after about twenty years we held a meeting at which I was unanimously voted head of department. Because I never spoke ill of anyone. Because I knew the history of every dead person in the necropolis. People consulted me – and still do – about so and so and this and that – they know that I know everything about the lives of the deceased, to the very last detail. I was a walking computer; just press the button and I'd come out with everything: day, month, year, hour, circumstances of death. Appointing me head of department was a joke, in any case: it's the only department there is here. Basically, I was still head of human resources, except that I don't get to choose the dead, and therefore have no power to throw them out if they do something seriously wrong. I try just to welcome newbies like yourself, help them to see things more clearly, and above all dissuade them from mis-using their second life, from doing something irrevocable, in search of revenge. . .'

Prosper Milandou seems out of breath. He comes over to you and leans back against the tree too, so you're sitting back to back, with just the trunk of the mango between you.

'You need to know there's another boss above me, called Black Mamba. . .'

You turn round to meet his eye:

'Where? I need to speak to him urgently and explain. . .'

'That would be a silly mistake; I get the feeling you want to return to the living. But I've just been telling you what a bad idea that is, from my own experience. . .'

As Prosper Milandou has his back to the entrance to the cemetery, he is unaware of the sight now occupying your attention: an old lady entering the burial ground. She advances haltingly, as though hesitating.

Without moving, Prosper Milandou says in a reassuring voice:

'An elderly lady. . . She's coming this way, by the look of it.'

The old lady is carrying two bunches of flowers. A white scarf covers her head.

At length Prosper Milandou turns towards you and says quietly:

'She's called Mâ Mapassa. Remember it. She's an important person here in Frère-Lachaise. . .'

Mâ Mapassa

———

A DRIED-UP WOMAN, OF AVERAGE HEIGHT, Mâ Mapassa seemed to carry the weight of the world of the living on her stooped back.

'Mâ Mapassa is a brave woman, but she'll never get over the death of her twins, a little girl and boy, savagely murdered by their uncle. The murderer's name was Jérémie Ndoki, the boss of the Mbota district, a part of Pointe-Noire I'm sure you know – the Babembé live there. People have more faith in fetishes there than they do in the law of the land. You're a Bembé, I guess you must have been there?'

Without waiting for your reply, Prosper Milandou continues:

'It's chaos down there in Mbota. The sorcerers deal in souls in broad daylight, at small markets. People think they're buying beef or sheep meat, and set off home with human flesh! It's madness! In the past the sorcerers at least had the decency to meet among themselves, in their own world, at dead of night, and would swap the souls of their near and dear ones for souls from families of other sorcerers, who came from far away, by plane, though not the kind of planes we see flying up above; theirs have giant bat wings and go much faster. If you're not initiated as a sorcerer you can't see them. Mbota became a magnet for ne'er-do-wells from the interior, there's even an airport there for their kind of plane. Whenever I hear the word Mbota it's like I'm seeing that bastard Jérémie Ndoki in the very act of poisoning his niece and nephew, just to get his hands on two positions at once: mayor of Pointe-Noire and president of the Kouilou region! That way he would be sure not only of controlling the local oil supply but also of filling his own pockets, thanks to some shady deals on the public markets...'

'I didn't know about this crime...'

'You were probably still in pull-up nappies at the time! When newbies ask me about these crimes, I always start by saying it was a double drama that took place two months before the municipal and regional elections. Jérémie Ndoki had gone to pick up his niece and nephew from his sister, Mama Mapassa, supposedly to buy them Christmas presents. He took them to the expensive shops in the city centre – if you ever see a black like you and me shopping there, they're bound to be a doctor, a lawyer, a bank manager or a minister. He bought a big pink teddy for his niece, and a blue bicycle for his nephew, then the three of them sat down at a table at Chez Gaspard, a stone's throw from the Grand Marché. That's where the poisoning took place, in cahoots with a cook who'd been paid a large sum by Jérémie Ndoki.

'As the late December afternoon drew to a close, the uncle took the kids back to their mother's. He left them a bit of pocket money and hugged them for a long while. The poison only began to work much later, in the middle of the night, at the hour when dogs see ghosts and keep them away by barking desperately till the first sign of daybreak. It's a kind of poison found only in the most obscure corners of Bouenza, like Tsiaki, Kinkouambala, Dzana, Tsomono or Moussanda, the home village of Mâ Mapassa and Jérémie Ndoki himself.

It devours the body slowly, a virus that circulates in your body for ten hours or more before killing you in one fell blow. Once dead, the victims turn green, their tongue turns blue, and their eyes bulge out of their head as though they had seen some terrifying creature. Rather than rotting they dry out like salted fish on the Tié-Tié market. You can imagine, the twins had stomach pains all night long, vomiting, yelling and screaming that they were being attacked by giant shadows. At first Mâ Mapassa thought they were having the usual kind of strange turn associated with twins. The girl and boy were both prone to feigning illness, worrying their mother with their fevers, headaches or unimportant little bumps and bruises. When the girl was sick, the boy would be sicker. And in a sense they were the same being, two bodies occupied by the same spirit. Apparently each of them only had one lung and the two took turns breathing, one exhaling, the other inhaling, and vice versa. But this time there was no pretence about it. Since bringing them into this world, Mâ Mapassa had never seen her little ones look green like this, turning with each passing hour into veritable mummies. They were rushed to the Adolphe-Cissé hospital. The twins were still fighting, squeezing hands, supporting each other to the last. They had already lost the power of speech, their eyes had tipped back in their sockets, their bodies were shivering, though the whole of the south of the country was in the grip of a heatwave. Everyone agreed the two little ones were fighting with great courage and still had a chance of pulling through. The daughter recovered her voice and was able to report on this slight improvement to her brother. But at six in the morning, when their uncle appeared at the door of their hospital room with even more presents – a plastic fire truck and a black Barbie doll – the two children screamed as one, pointing at him:

"'It's him! The devil that came to the house yesterday looked just like him!"

'They turned from green to dark blue, and were by now almost frozen solid. Again they lost their voices, as a cock in the distance crowed three times, the sky grew dark and a gentle rain began to fall. The twins' eyes closed for all eternity...'

Mâ Mapassa stands still for a few seconds, then sets off walking again, her eyes fixed on her feet, never once looking behind her or ahead.

'When she stops,' Prosper Milandou tells you, 'it's to avoid treading on an ant or any other insect. She respects all life, including the little creatures that get crushed by people, accidentally or on purpose...'

She makes her way over to a grave at the far end, close to the wall.

Prosper Milandou flicks off a fly that has just settled on his chin and begins:

'After the death of the twins the city of Pointe-Noire was aware their uncle had consulted one of the Mbota sorcerers in order to gain power, and that the sorcerer had revealed to him that what he sought was in the gift of the two children. Blood was required, a great deal of blood, so a double sacrifice, and a colossal sum of money, which the uncle had to pay in cash up front. The sorcerer explained that the sacrifice of the girl twin would give him the direction of the city, and that of the boy twin would install him at the head of the Kouilou region, and that was how most politicians and tribal chiefs of this country went about things. He encouraged him, all the same, to curb his greed, and sacrifice just one of the children. To make a choice between the town hall and the region. The sorcerer was ready to accept just half the sum, but Jérémie Ndoki had not the slightest hesitation and replied that he couldn't imagine not holding both positions at the same time. The sorcerer washed his hands in a bowl of warm water in front of Jérémie Ndoki. This was to indicate his rejection of any responsibility for the eventual consequences. From now on it was up to the uncle to decide in all conscience whether to put his plan into action or renounce his desire for power. Obviously he opted to proceed, and the sorcerer pocketed the million CFA francs before preparing the poison that he himself dubbed "zero fault", for its efficacy.'

He's interrupted by the same fly that bothered him a few minutes earlier. He freezes, like a cat, catches the insect on his shoulder and stuffs it in his mouth.

'It was asking for it!'

He doesn't even leave you time to conceal your disgust:

'Where was I? Oh yes, Ndoki ended up poisoning his niece and his nephew and after the death of the twins, Pointe-Noire became accursed in the eyes of the whole country. Whenever a Pontenegrin went to another town or village, they'd hear the words: "Ah, you're from Pointe-Noire, the place where they kill twin children for power." Pontenegrins got called every name under the sun, and were even run out of town by people shaking sticks and throwing stones. Jérémie Ndoki brought disgrace on every inhabitant of Pointe-Noire. In an attempt to salvage their image, they gave the children a farewell ceremony unlike any other. As far as I know it was the longest funeral ever held for anyone in this town, including the one held for the honourable politician Jean Félix-Tchicaya, in 1961. It lasted ten days and ten nights! There were so many people. They said spirits had come from every forest throughout the land to pay tribute to the two little angels and open the pathway to Heaven for them, where they would be seated at the right hand of the Lord! Women, men, children all lined up, from the most distant districts of the city to outside Mâ Mapassa's plot in the Rex Quarter, to see the little children one last time. The burial began very early in the morning and ended very late at night. The bars and other late-night venues were shut for the occasion, even though the government hadn't given the order for it. No music, no hooting of horns, no shagging or anything that might stand in the way of the children ascending to Heaven. Instead of a minute, the people observed an entire day of silence. The affair spread well beyond the boundaries of the town, even of the country: the radio stations in Cameroon, in the other Congo and in Central Africa spoke of it as though the twins had been born in their country. And the crowds went to the cemetery dressed all in white with T-shirts printed with the photo of the twins' smiling faces.

But their Uncle Jérémie did not step down. During the funeral his voice could still be heard on National Radio. He wept crocodile tears, urged the local population to turn out in droves to vote for him in memory of his niece and nephew, whom he claimed to love above all else. He explained now that he was standing in the elections with the aim of avenging all twins everywhere who had been victims of injustice and medical error – for in his view, the twins had died from the incompetence of the staff at the Adolphe-Cissé hospital. With that, I have to tell you, he went too far. Fired up by his cynical remarks, the Pontenegrins immediately went to smash up his villa near the Côte Sauvage, setting fire to his two designer cars, the only ones of their kind in the whole of Pointe-Noire: a Mercedes 280 and a Jaguar Mark 2. They caught Jérémie Ndoki just as he was trying to take a taxi to the border and reach Angola, probably hoping to disappear in Europe, where he had stashed most of his money. He was already safe inside the vehicle when the taxi driver did a U-turn and brought him back towards the seething crowd. The police saved his neck just in time: he had already been stripped and bound, and was being dragged towards the Côte Sauvage, to be thrown alive into the Atlantic Ocean. The over-excited mob got as far as the beach. Unfortunately, ten police vans had got there before them. Jérémie Ndoki had used his considerable influence to save the situation. But what was he to do with his life from now on? Surely he couldn't spend it slinking round the city streets! Granted, he enjoyed the protection of the police, but he would need to bribe these officials to secure their continuing support until such time as his double crime vanished from the collective memory. Year on year the appetite of the police expanded; they knew the politician had no choice. His sources of income had dried up since he had been relieved of his functions as chief of the Mbota district where, thanks to some shifty business with the sale of plots of land, he had become one of the richest men in Pointe-Noire. His wife and their three children had managed to take the Micheline train to Brazzaville, from where they had crossed the river and taken refuge in the other Congo. By the time three years were up, Jérémie Ndoki had given all his worldly goods to the police. Signs of his decline became clear when he gave them his shirts, trousers and watches, and his protectors abandoned him to his fate. He would have liked a trial, so he could at least get sent to prison, with a degree of security. No one was prepared to grant what would have been perceived as a favour. Jérémie Ndoki was by now a mere shadow of a man: no home, no cars, no work, no family. Pontenegrins no longer recognised him in the street. Barefoot, dressed in rags that scarcely hid his private parts, an unruly thatch of hair, flowing beard, he hung around begging in the city centre outside Score and Printania, where the occasional European would toss him a coin. Whenever a car stopped, he would rush up to clean the windscreen in hope of payment. A few years after the death of the twins he joined the group of crazies wandering naked along the Côte Sauvage. He learned their language and their ways. Nothing more was heard of him till one day a body was found, naked, lifeless, near the wharf. It was the corpse of Jérémie Ndoki. Did he die of natural causes? The question remains unanswered to this day. Many believe he took his own life to end his long suffering, his slow descent to Hell. Others that the twins rose from their grave to exact their own revenge, since their uncle's life was a requirement for them to gain eternal rest. I favour this interpretation myself: how else do you explain that the corpse of Jérémie Ndoki bore marks of strangulation? And also, there was something strange about the marks found round his neck: from the hands of two children. . .'

He coughs a little, and strokes his bead, breaking the short silence he's just observed – perhaps to get his breath back, or gather his recollections:

'Because that criminal, Jérémie Ndoki, was rich, people were betting he would naturally be buried over in the rich folk's cemetery. But there the dead organised an all-out strike, which every Pontenegrin still remembers. The spirits came out of their tombs in a state of revolt, and appeared at the market, in bars, restaurants, discotheques, at bus stops, at the entrance to the seaport, in hospitals, outside the Victory Palace and Atlantic Palace hotels, outside cinemas – the Rex, the Roy and the Duo – and even before the prostitutes in the Trois-Cents Quarter. They could melt into crowds, pass for normal people, and in order to get their message over they scrawled on many of the public buildings that they didn't want the murderer at the Cemetery of the Rich, and would burn the city down if he was thrust upon them. Pointe-Noire then experienced one of the longest rainfalls in its entire history. The Diosso volcano awoke from its centuries-long slumber, the sky seemed alight with fireworks and the Atlantic Ocean threw up waves as high as American sky-scrapers. Pentecostal and other churches seized on the occasion and announced that the end of days was nigh. Their congregations grew by thousands every day. Since the Cemetery of the Rich was opposed to receiving Jérémie Ndoki, some suggested him being buried here, where in principle there would be no problem. Yeah, right! We organised a general strike here too, after I was contacted by the bigwigs from the rich folk's cemetery. We don't wish to be on bad terms with them, as some of us get invited to their cemetery for the Independence Day festivities on 15 August, or on the Day of the Dead, 2 November, and even on the birthdays of some of the distinguished deceased from the mausoleum for the moneyed classes. I called a meeting of the cemetery elders and our guidelines were clear: "We must not accept that bastard Jérémie Ndoki here, this is not a dumping ground!" All the elders responded: "We won't let him in, and let's tell the whole world about it!" They were so angry, torrential rain fell upon the town, followed by a heatwave that melted the tarmac on the major roads, and the metal sheets on our roofs. The situation was getting worse by the day. His Excellency Théophile-Florent Tsiba de Montaigne, the charismatic MP and chief advisor to President Papa Mokonzi Ayé alias Zarathustra, wrote an eloquent and compelling letter to the nation's leader. The document was leaked, a photocopy fell into the hands of a great number of Congolese, but I can quote the remarks of His Excellency Théophile-Florent Tsiba de Montaigne from memory:

"'Monsieur le Président, for several days now I have been making precise notes in order to keep you informed of the strike by the dead currently rocking Pointe-Noire, and spreading across the country. One's first reaction is that it is ridiculous – which is precisely what makes it dangerous, threatening to exceed even what the French experienced in May 1968, when your illustrious and distinguished homologue, Général de Gaulle, left France for twenty-four hours for a discreet trip to Baden-Baden, to ask his wartime friend Massu for advice, while France burned! The following year, moreover, your illustrious and distinguished homologue was forced to submit to a humiliating referendum which he himself had called, thus putting his position in peril. In the event of a 'no', your illustrious and distinguished homologue promised to resign. And indeed, the French people did vote 'no', and the general hid himself away in his home village of Colombey-les-Deux-Églises to write your bedtime reading, his 'War Memoirs', dying a year later from a heart attack!

"'Mr President, there has never been a referendum in your country, and you are right to be cautious. The Congolese never understand simple questions; they always give complicated answers, which are actually questions in disguise, and this time the questions will all be about when you are going to resign, as your illustrious and distinguished French homologue did before you. Besides, if we're being realistic about our country, we know even the dead will try to spoil the results, and believe me, they won't vote for you – they're not afraid of you any more; their world is not your world! Today the public basically considers that if, in a referendum of that sort, we don't cheat with France's blessing – which we will get, or we'll give our oil to the Americans – we might as well pack our bags and seek asylum in a neighbouring country or in Europe, where you too, if you're lucky, can write your war memoirs and die of a heart attack.

"'Mr President, I don't believe that's what you want. In order to win the situation back in our favour, I propose to write you a historic speech, the envy of the entire world, which will draw on the subtle thought of the great sage of Mali, Amadou Hampâté Bâ: when two lizards face each other on a ceiling with a mosquito net strung beneath them and a burning oil lamp close by, it is likely that the two creatures, as they slip and fall, will cause a fire, leading to a mortal drama in the household. This one little squabble between two lizards is where we must at all costs intervene, Mr President. We do not know who the strikers lurking in the shadows really are, and some of them may have infiltrated the government. In the course of a cabinet meeting you may believe you are sitting opposite members of your government, when in fact you are surrounded by grouchy dead people who will sweep you off with them into the world beyond. For this reason, Mr President, I have taken the precaution of summoning ten sorcerers from your native village to come and make sure that none of your current ministers are ghosts, and, if need be, to put to death by hanging any phantom-cum-ministers they may find. If we fail to act quickly the opposition will turn the situation to their advantage, and that's how regime change starts, Mr President!

"'I know, Mr President, that Jérémie Ndoki was a childhood friend of yours; you were at primary school together, and collège, and lycée, and you must have been very attached to him to have turned a blind eye to most of his shady dealings in Pointe-Noire. However, Mr President, in politics friendship stops when it comes to saving your own slice of Camembert. You must therefore cancel your official visit to the President of Cameroon, Paul Biya, and address the nation, condemning the idea that Jérémie Ndoki be interred in the rich folk's cemetery. Nor does he belong in the poor folk's cemetery, at Frère-Lachaise. This is what you need to say to the people: 'I say to you now, with a clear conscience and of serene mind, looking Congo straight in the eye: Jérémie Ndoki belongs not in a cemetery, but in Hell!' Don't worry, Mr President, we'll find a place to bury your childhood buddy. We'll get his wife and children over from the other Congo, and the affair can be settled once and for all. If you think about it, the population will applaud you, and the family of Jérémie Ndoki and all their people will be eternally grateful to you too. This is the only way we can turn round this popular uprising and catch the opposition by surprise, Mr President!'"

The department manager broke off at this point, clearly pleased his memory had not let him down during his recital of the letter written by His Excellency Théophile-Florent Tsiba de Montaigne. He shut his eyes for a few seconds, opened them again and resumed:

'President Papa Mokonzi Ayé alias Zarathustra seemed unconvinced. He asked His Excellency Théophile-Florent Tsiba de Montaigne:

'"How credible is your story about the cemetery and Hell, though? I feel it needs something really strong at the end. How about I go all out to impress the spirits, if I end with something like: 'Thus spake Zarathustra!?'"

'His Excellency Théophile-Florent Tsiba de Montaigne replied calmly:

'"Keep it plain and simple, Mr President. People will start asking who this Zarathustra is, it could backfire on you. Besides, it's you speaking, the President of the Republic, not this Zarathustra guy!"

'In the end the Head of State spoke just before the evening news. He regurgitated to the letter what His Excellency Théophile-Florent Tsiba de Montaigne had written for him, and ended with the resounding words:

'"In his story 'No quarrel is ever small', the great sage of Mali, Amadou Hampâté Bâ, warned us: a conflict, however negligible, should be resolved immediately! As father of the nation, responsible for the souls of the dead, the living, the still-to-be-born and the should-have-been-born, I owe it to myself to take a historic decision from which there will be no turning back. I say to you now, with clear conscience and untroubled mind: Jérémie Ndoki belongs not in a cemetery, but in Hell! Thus spake Zarathustra!"

'From that day forward, the people began to call him Papa Mokonzi Ayé alias Zarathustra. The next day, at dead of night, two black cars came to pick up Jérémie Ndoki's body from the Adolphe-Cissé morgue and conveyed it to his native village, which, since the rural exodus, numbered no more than two hundred or so inhabitants, most of them old people. The wife and children of the deceased reached the village by crossing the Congo river, then taking a helicopter laid on for them by President Zarathustra himself. It is also said that the president attended the hastily organised funeral. A week later, ten of the president's sorcerers were brought before the ministers' cabinet to sniff out ministers suspected of being evil spirits. They were all southerners who had been to top French universities. They were hanged at first light, and replaced by northerners, all of the same ethnicity as the president. Some time later we heard that the grave of Jérémie Ndoki had been defiled, and the body was no longer inside it. Could anyone actually have cared less?'

Prosper Milandou's tone suddenly altered, and he said quietly:

'And for more than three decades, that woman you see, Mâ Mapassa, has been coming to this cemetery every weekend to lay a bunch of flowers for each of her beloved children! I have never seen her face close-up. Even if a bomb went off behind her, she wouldn't turn around. All she cares about is not stepping on insects. And she has an eagle eye for them! Watch carefully – she'll go over and place the flowers on the children's grave, pray for about a quarter of an hour, then leave, with her chin still pressed close to her chest...

Mâ Mapassa has gone past you both now. She heads for the middle of the cemetery, lays the two bouquets with great care on the twins' tomb.

She has just knelt to pray. Even from here you can hear her murmuring words, and sobbing.

After the quarter hour for which Prosper Milandou bade you keep silent, the old lady comes back this way again.

She mumbles very softly:

'Good day to you, Monsieur Director of Human Resources. . . and good day to you too, newcomer. . .'

Prosper Milandou bows deeply in response. You do the same. He wipes away a tear, and the woman is already gone from Frère-Lachaise.

'You're weeping, sir?'

'Could you be a little less formal?'

You try, and say: 'You're weeping, my friend?'

'Oh, yes. Even in here we sometimes weep.'

'So can she see us? How old is she?'

'She's a mother of twins, and mothers of twins see everything. . . I've no idea how old she is, but everyone thinks she carries the weight of a whole century on her shoulders.'

He seems to be in a hurry now, he's glancing left and right.

'Well, don't let me keep you, I've done what I had to do. You can see things as they are now, you've got your own spot. I suggest you rest. Time passes slowly here; a day in life here is months in the life of the living, sometimes even a year. I'm dead on my feet now; I partied too hard on 15 August and the days afterwards, with my friends in the rich folk's cemetery. They know how to have a good time! They have wine that comes direct from France. They're buried with it, and when they run out their families bring them more! So they're drunk from Monday through Sunday, twenty-four hours a day. Yesterday a fight nearly broke out across the cemetery. I put a stop to no fewer than four altercations, some row about an affair that never got sorted while the deceased were still living. The woman is actually still alive, and remarried to a third scoundrel, but her real husband and her lover are both dead, still fighting it out between them whenever they have a drink too many. . . But that's another story; if I get into that we'll be here for all eternity!'

You don't reply. He admits, with a guilty air:

'Yes, I know, I talk too much. Black Mamba has often said so. . .'

He turns his back to you, moves a few steps away, as though he's leaving, but suddenly turns round and comes back:

'Oh, I almost forgot: are you free next weekend?'

'I don't know.'

'You're not going to keep on and on walking round your grave in deep despair! I can introduce you to my friends at the rich folk's cemetery; that's how it works, by co-option, otherwise they'll never open the door to you. . .'

'No, I have to go into town first, I have things to sort out and I—'

'You want revenge, do you?'

'Well, in theory I wasn't meant to die that night and—'

'That's what the dead always say, like criminals shouting that they're innocent even when the proof is overwhelming! I've already told you, it's like in life, you only die once, you'll end up regretting it. . .'

He gives you one last look and murmurs, before vanishing in a great cloud of dust that hides him from view:

'Pity, I thought you looked like an intelligent guy, but I was wrong!'

In the blink of an eye the dust cloud is gone, and all trace of Prosper Milandou with it. . .

The Artist

———

YOU'RE STILL SITTING under your mango tree, you haven't left it; you're wondering if this is really the moment to venture beyond the cemetery walls. Flurries of wind shake the leaves of your tree and a few mangoes fall to the ground, a few small reptiles come to feed on the rotting mangoes, then vanish down their holes around the grave.

A tiny old man, hunched, with a red hat and shoulder bag. He reaches the foot of your tree, hastily grabs the mangoes and stuffs them into his bag, without asking your permission.

'What are you up to, sir?' you ask him.

'It's the only mango tree in the whole cemetery, so it belongs to everyone, otherwise you have to go outside, and people on the outside are so horrible to us. . .'

You detect an unpleasant smell. *The little guy needs a shower,* you think. He is barefoot, his nails like mountain ridges. Strands of his hair trail from under his hat, like long twists of creeper. In the popular districts he'd get taken for a rasta come down from the mountain after years spent meditating, living among wild creatures.

'Why would you go into town? You only die once. . . When we're dead we're dead!'

Surprised, you retort:

'How do you know? Are you Black Mamba, the boss around here?'

'No, I'm not Black Mamba... But he knows where you are, where you should be, where I am, where I should be. He knows everything.'

'So who are you then, sir?'

'Oh, please, Prosper Milandou already told you, no formalities here. I am the Artist.'

'The Artist? Which artist?'

'I'm Lully Madeira, the incomparable, the one and only, the eternal and unique Lully Madeira, this earth will never see his like, for the Almighty made only one, who is unique in all the universe, end of story!'

The name rings a bell. Yes, of course, you remember now. The old gardener from the Victory Palace hotel, George Moutaka, used to tell you the strange tale of Lully Madeira. The gardener claimed to have seen him several times when rehearsing with his band, African Flash, at the Touco Mambo Club in the Rex Quarter. George Moutaka's house was next door to the hall. Hence he could claim proudly to have seen the Artist 'with his own eyes'.

The Touco Mambo Club hall only held three hundred and fifty people, the authorities threatened to close it if they went over that. But they often did exceed the limit because the owner, a Lebanese tradeswoman, greased the palm of the head of staff at the Mairie to get him to turn a blind eye.

Before rehearsals and concerts a host would bellow:

'Lully Madeira, the incomparable, the one and only, the eternal and unique Lully Madeira, this earth will never see his like, for the Almighty made only one, who is unique in all the universe, end of story!'

The percussionist beat his set, the drummer practically

broke his sticks as the dancers scattered across the podium, dressed in red with sequined mini-skirts. The percussionist took off his shirt, the bass player too. And at this moment, swore George Moutaka, the solo guitarist Lokounia, alias Jimi Hendrix, the best-known member of the group after Lully Madeira, played the strings of his guitar with his teeth to make the sound of a motorbike starting up!

Then the four singers appeared, in order of size.

By now there was red smoke everywhere in the hall. Everything was hidden, then when the smoke disappeared upwards, the host would shout again:

'Lully Madeira! Lully Madeira! Lully Madeira! The incomparable, the one and only, the eternal and unique Lully Madeira, this earth will never see his like, for the Almighty made only one, who is unique in all the universe, end of story!'

There was Lully Madeira in the centre of the podium, two singers to his left, two to his right, the dancers behind. With all the smoke, you couldn't tell that the Artist was a hunchback, but once it cleared you became aware of the huge hump that pulled his whole body over to the right and was the source of his great fame. His fans claimed he deliberately sang 'off to one side', when in fact it was the weight of his hump.

According to George Moutaka, the Pontenegrins were well aware that at the start of Lully Madeira's career with his band he hadn't been a hunchback at all. Back then young girls didn't faint during his concerts and rehearsals, the mothers from the Grand Marché didn't give him mangoes, mandarins, pineapples or papayas, even though some of his songs got played on the radio. Everything changed the year he consulted a feticheur, furious that rival groups such as Yoko Lokole or Coyabilé were topping the bill in the city and getting their songs played night and day on the radio. What did they have that he and African Flash didn't have? he wondered, while endlessly criticising his rivals' albums, with 'these insipid and badly written songs'.

Lully Madeira had gone to consult Denzou, a famous feticheur originally from Bouenza, where you don't fool about making little amulets. In any face-off between ethnic groups, people fear the people of Bouenza. They keep amulets stuffed in their pants to help them win at war; it makes them invincible. Machine-gun bullets fly straight past them; they are transformed into wild creatures, trees, mountains, dead wood, bush fire or torrential rain. They act in a variety of different ways, such as putting spells on people, manipulating the thoughts of a married woman or man so they'll seek a divorce, bringing back a woman or man who has run away from their marriage, attracting wealth, success, it just depends what you want.

Feticheur Denzou had warned Lully Madeira:

'It's going to cost you. . .'

Lully Madeira laughed. He'd come with a black plastic bag full of notes:

'All that's for you, and it's just an advance! I'm playing Monday to Sunday at the Touco Mambo Club, I'll give you fifty per cent of the takings. . .'

Denzou replied:

'You haven't understood what I'm saying, Lully. . .'

'How much do you want then? Don't be embarrassed, just tell me. . .'

'Spirits are not attracted by the kind of money humans make. What interests them is finding a body to inhabit, because there's not much room left now underground or up in the sky.'

'How would they inhabit a body?'

'You just have to agree to take one in. I contact them to discuss it, I sign a contract in your name. . .'

'Well, if that's all there is to it, contact them straightaway!'

'You still don't get it, Lully. When they inhabit your body, you'll get this huge lump on your back. . .'

'No! Can't you see – I'm a looker, I'm elegant!'

'Leave me alone then. I'm busy. Go and work for your success.'

As soon as he stepped out of Denzou's place, a little voice murmured that he had blown his only chance of attaining success in life. Another voice urged him to compare his situation with that of the town's other artists. He was pretty sure they must have signed contracts with the spirits, that was why their records were in the hit parade of the Voice of the Congolese Revolution or of Voice of Congo-Zaire. These musicians clearly weren't hunchbacks but had perhaps signed pacts to shelter spirits in other parts of their bodies. They had all made a sacrifice of some kind. Tchico Litoyi was blind. Fernand Kobalana had a weak right foot. Firmine Pembey couldn't have any more children. And what did they all have in common? Their lightning rise to fame.

Lully Madeira swiftly turned on his heels and went back to plead with Denzou:

'Ok, I agree to house some spirits in my back!'

'Absolutely sure?'

'I've never once been in the hit parade, though I know I'm better than those jokers whose discs sell like hot cakes! It's time to right this wrong. . .'

'Success will come. I guarantee. . .'

Lully Madeira listened with interest to the promises of Denzou, who arranged to meet him at the cemetery in the Voungou district at midnight, the other side of the Tchinouka river. . .

George Moutaka went on with his tale with all the confidence of the eyewitness, swearing that Denzou and Lully Madeira had sat down together on the oldest tomb in the

Voungou cemetery while the moon peered down on them from up above. After explaining that he was going now, and that someone else would come and speak to him, Denzou abandoned the musician in this sinister place and vanished in the twilight.

The Artist heard a deep, trembling voice:

'Are you Lully Madeira?'

'Yes, that's me, Lully Madeira, leader of the band African Flash. . .'

'I'm the oldest inhabitant of the cemetery, I represent all the spirits, and am empowered to speak in their name.'

'But I can't see you?'

'We are not of the same world. I see you. Is this your final decision? Are you quite sure?'

'I've thought it over, I swear. I've already told Denzou. . .'

'Think some more. The owls are watching, they are witness to the agreements humans sign with us. . .'

'I am ready. I swear.'

In the same authoritative tone, the gardener described how the owls came to settle on the branches of the filao trees surrounding the Voungou cemetery. They hooted the news in the deepest hours of the night, and the spirits gathered together at three in the morning while Lully Madeira lay in a coma.

When the Artist opened his eyes again, it was already five in the morning. He couldn't get up, his body seemed to lean with its entire weight to the right, and he was unable to straighten up as he could before. So at first he tried moving, hopping like a little goat, then staggering, like a praying mantis. Not until he reached the exit to the cemetery did he find a new way of walking: hopping on his left foot, then dragging his right foot up level with the left. . .

Arriving at his house in the Rex Quarter around six in the morning, Lully Madeira slept for the rest of the day. In the evening he heard insistent knocking and went over to the door, still hopping, then staggering. The three musicians from his band did not recognise him, and were somewhat scared by the character looking out at them.

The backing vocalist, Penky, was most frightened:

'Sorry to disturb, are you one of our boss's parents? He's expected at the Touco Mambo Club. There are people there already who've paid to come to rehearsals, there may be a fight if we don't rehearse!'

'Penky, it's me! I'm Lully Madeira! The incomparable, the one and only, the eternal and unique Lully Madeira, this earth will never see his like, for the Almighty made only one, who is unique in all the universe, end of story!'

The musicians had been about to run away, but they recognised his way of speaking and the long slogan, which only the Artist could deliver quite like that, almost as though singing.

But Penky was still worried.

'Chief, you're sick, you've had an accident. We'll take you to the hospital...'

'Me? Sick? Lully Madeira – sick?'

'Just lie down and rest. I've stood in for you before, I can do it again...'

'No one can replace Lully Madeira! I'll come with you at once to the rehearsal!'

'Chief, people in the street will see the state you're in; they'll say—'

'Who's going to see me? We'll take a taxi!'

The Artist took longer than usual to change. Only the red pullover, being very stretchy, fitted over the contours of his hump; his cotton shirts were all too tight. He slipped on a pair of red jersey trousers that fit snugly round his thighs, polished red shoes with a side buckle. None of the musicians spoke as they made their way, each still wondering if this man with the hunchback really was Lully Madeira...

Penky brought the Artist in by the back door of the Touco

Mambo Club and said to his other colleagues, 'I don't want the public to see him now, or they'll start pelting us with rotten mangoes.'

Lully Madeira sat down in a corner lit only by a little candle. From a distance he looked like a turtle struggling to lay an egg. But he was in a trance, frenetically scribbling something on a piece of paper.

When he heard his musicians warming up the room with the song 'Try to Remember' by Nana Mouskouri, he leapt onto the podium like a kangaroo, shaking off Penky, who had tried to restrain him:

'What is that? Why are you playing old French hits? Stop that right now!'

The public, surprised to see this stooped old man, all burst out laughing, then called out:

'Boo! Boo! Clear off, Quasimodo!'

Lully Madeira said to Penky, 'Listen carefully: from now on, no more covers of songs from France or Zaire. I'm a genius, and you'd better believe it! I've just written three songs in ten minutes and that's what we'll practise today! I'll write twenty more before the big Christmas concert...'

At this Penky knew it was all over with the band. Lully Madeira actually believed he had talent.

He was on his feet now, giving instructions to the drummer and solo guitarist, Lokounia alias Jimi Hendrix. He had asked the backing singers to quickly go and take up their positions onstage, and as soon as they were in place, Lully Madeira leapt into the centre of the stage and, facing his instrumentalists, yelled:

'ONE! TWO! THREE!'

At first the band was all over the place, to the alarm of the overcrowded room:

'Where's Lully Madeira? Where's he gone? We don't want this Quasimodo! If Lully Madeira doesn't show we'll smash the place up!'

Without turning a whisker, the hunchback took the microphone in his right hand and began singing, his eyes lifted skywards. Was he speaking with angels? With God? Was he playing an imaginary gig in Paradise? Whatever, the booing had stopped. A voice of such beauty had never been heard in Pointe-Noire! The hunchback's lyrics spoke of how lovely, how wonderful, Pointe-Noire was, with the Atlantic Ocean, the Côte Sauvage, the bars with packed terraces, the twenty-four-hours-a-day atmosphere, and so on. And to top it all, he gave the city a nickname: 'Ponton-la-Belle'.

That day, George Moutaka confirmed, girls were fainting all over the Touco Mambo Club, and had to be revived by having ice-cold Primus beer thrown in their faces. Who did not shed a tear? Penky was crying too and lost his voice, leaving Lully Madeira to lead the choruses with the other vocalists, who answered him as though they had sung the song a thousand times before. . .

At the end of the rehearsal, the hunchback stepped forward towards the crowd and in a voice of angelic purity, as though he wished to introduce the new Lully Madeira, risen from the ashes of the old one, he said:

'Good evening. I am Lully Madeira, the leader of the band African Flash. I wrote the song you heard twenty minutes ago. . . It's called "Ponton-la-Belle", and is a tribute to our town, Pointe-Noire, the finest city in the world. . .'

The next day the Voice of the Congolese Revolution invited African Flash into their studio to record their song 'Ponton-la-Belle'. They played it all day long, from Monday through Sunday, for a year, on the show *Songs on Demand*. Other bands played it too, cover versions. It was translated into every language in the country and also those of Zaire. 'Ponton-la-Belle' stayed in the hit parade of the Congo and Zaire for a whole year.

Lully Madeira and his band were now famous. They had a crazy year, with posters at every crossroads in town. The

Artist could no longer move around town without causing interminable traffic jams. All the talk was of his group, of him, and on the front cover of magazines he was always surrounded by beautiful girls. His success grew and grew; every song shot to number one in the hit parade. Lully Madeira's cup was running over; he had reached the heady heights he'd always yearned for and crushed his competitors, who were caught short by his sensational success.

George Moutaka appeared to grow sad as he explained that although this extraordinary episode had propelled African Flash onto the national scene in record time, things actually went rather too fast, and whenever things zoom skywards they tend to plummet back down at a similar speed. The musicians now quarrelled among themselves, usually over women, or because they all wanted to sing on Lully Madeira's right-hand side, so as to be more visible and make it clear that they would become leader of the band the day the boss died. Fans began to notice these tensions at their concerts and during rehearsals: they played robotically, without giving any sign of pleasure at having stirred up such a commotion throughout the land. Lully Madeira yelled at them and threw cans of beer in their faces. You'd hear him shouting that these artists would be nothing without him, he was God's elect, it was all thanks to his talent that they'd achieved all this.

And then, overnight, after a year of mounting success, he announced to his musicians that he was breaking up the band and going solo. From now on he would work with independent musicians, chosen by himself to accompany him on tour or when recording albums. Having sacked everyone, he then brought out a new album which he'd recorded in Zaire. He appeared on the album cover, smiling broadly, wearing a gold crown on his head. The songs were played in nightclubs, on buses, in markets, at marriage celebrations and wakes. Some people said it was his best album ever; not to say the album of the decade, though Lully Madeira set the record straight in interviews, calling it the album of the century. Some of his more nostalgic fans looked back with longing to the old era of African Flash and accused the Artist of having fallen into the trap of commercial music, 'like other mediocrities'. Even so, young bands were inspired by his rhythms, covering his songs, imitating the way he moved, with his hump, convinced that Lully Madeira's marvellous voice came from his infirmity and that hunchbacks naturally had amazing voices, since the sound was initially purified by passing through their protuberance, the better to caress the ears of their waiting fans. . .

George Moutaka assumed a solemn air as he came to Lully Madeira's twilight years. Despite enjoying a decade of success, the singer was obsessed with one idea only: to play at the Olympia, the venue where all the world's greats had performed. As far as he knew the only Congolese ever to have played there was Tabu Ley Rochereau, and even then only as Johnny Hallyday's support. So Lully Madeira would be the first black African to play the mythical Parisian venue. To this end he went to the Victory Palace hotel, in the city centre, to meet with a white producer who worked for one of the big record labels in Europe. The producer promised to make him famous throughout the world, and to open the doors of the Olympia to him, since he was a personal friend of the director, Bruno Coquatrix.

A day before this crucial meeting, Lully Madeira went back to consult with Denzou, who warned him on no account to meet with the white man.

'It's the Devil tempting you. You're famous here in Brazzaville, let that be enough. The white man you're going to meet isn't a real white. . . The spirits always end up punishing the greedy and they've had their eye on you for a while now. They're determined to move out of the little house on your back; they're appalled by your behaviour. Up till now they've been pretty much on your side. . .'

Lully Madeira ignored Denzou's advice. The spirits were displeased by his sacking his African Flash musicians, who had since fallen on hard times, playing guitars in the streets of Pointe-Noire or begging, while their former boss continued to live the high life. . .

The Artist went to the city centre in his Citroën CX, which his fans recognised from a distance; it was one of only a handful in Pointe-Noire. He brought with him to the meeting with the European producer a large bag full of his new recordings, and his old cassettes and discs. After parking his car on the boulevard du Général Charles de Gaulle, he continued on foot to the rue de Bouvanzi which leads to the Victory Palace hotel, hoping to be met by cheering crowds – it was in such moments of collective furore that he felt truly loved. He dreamed of the scale of his international success, with his photo and posters on the walls of the principal cities of Europe. He chuckled happily, skipping a little, whistling the tune of a new song, inevitably a future hit, and didn't even notice an ancient Pontenegrin Transport Company bus arriving at breakneck speed – the driver had lost all control, despite several attempts to brake. Too late: Lully Madeira's little body was tossed into the air and landed on the opposite side of Bouenza Street, less than three hundred metres from where his meeting was due to take place, surrounded now by an ever-growing crowd of people weeping as though they had lost one of their own family. . .

A month of national mourning was announced on the radio. President Papa Mokonzi Ayé alias Zarathustra and his government all came to Pointe-Noire for the funeral. After the month of mourning the mayor of the city decided that a giant statue should be erected to Lully Madeira on the spot where the bus had run him over, and that from now on, two days before Christmas, a joyful celebration would be held in his memory. The people of Pointe-Noire were pleased by the mayor's offer of a house to each of Lully Madeira's former band members. Without them would the musician have become a household name? African Flash started rehearsing again at the Touco Mambo Club, with Penky as their leader. They never achieved the success of Lully Madeira's day, but nor did they seek to increase their audience by consulting sorcerer Denzou.

On the day Lully Madeira was buried at Frère-Lachaise – he could have rightfully been laid to rest at the rich folk's cemetery, but was denied this privilege because he had signed a pact with the Devil – the Pontenegrins dressed all in white and lined up along the rue du Repos, imitating the hunched stance of the Artist. They sang 'Ponton-la-Belle' in the version of Penky and African Flash. The mayor gave a funeral oration on the radio, saying that even though Lully Madeira had made a pact with the evil spirits, he would remain forever in people's hearts, his legend would never die.

George Moutaka always ended his story with tears in his eyes, and you knew that he'd tell it over again if anyone dared say they didn't know who Lully Madeira was. To get him to tell it you had only to say:

'This Lully Madeira, did he really exist, or is it just some story people your age like to tell?'

The old man would leap to his feet, looking suddenly much younger than his years, and immediately impersonate the Artist:

'I'm Lully Madeira! The incomparable, the one and only, the eternal and unique Lully Madeira, this earth will never see his like, for the Almighty made only one, who is unique in all the universe, end of story!'

Lully Madeira looks at you with a secretive smile, as though he knows you knew all along who he was, despite your youth:

'People will tell you all sorts of nonsense,' he says, defensively, 'but hear this once and for all: I am Lully Madeira! The incomparable, the one and only, the eternal and unique Lully Madeira, this earth will never see his like, for the Almighty made only one, who is unique in all the universe, end of story!'

Will he spend his entire death spouting the self-promotional slogan of God's chosen Artist?

He puts his shoulder bag back on after picking up a few more mangoes. Perhaps he is trying to make up for earlier.

'Shall I leave some for you?'

'No, thank you. I'm not hungry.'

'Why not? You haven't eaten since you died, what's that about? You'll be all skin and bone!'

You're not quite sure it's a joke, but he's cackling like a true hunchback:

'He, he he!' Don't you mind me, it's just gallows humour, we always try it on with the newbies.'

He moves away from your grave a little and vanishes in a thick cloud of dust.

Just as you start to see a little more clearly, all trace of Lully Madeira is gone...

The Old Man and the Book

———

AS SOON AS THE CLOUD OF DUST carries off the Artist, another person appears to you, no bigger than the last. He is thin, face as flat as a fish, with bushy eyebrows, a grey beard and red, bulging eyes. He moves unnaturally slowly, setting one foot after the other on the ground.

He has just closed the book in his hands and is putting it away in a pocket of his ragged clothing that trails behind him on the ground. Now he's taking a walk around your grave.

'I've come to bring you to your senses,' he says.

'Are you Black Mamba, sir, the famous boss of this place?'

He doubles up laughing.

'Please, drop the formalities – Prosper Milandou and the Artist already told you!'

'Are you the famous Black Mamba?'

'Famous? Let's not exaggerate, such language belongs to the living. . . Let's just say that I know everything that happens here, where you are, where you're meant to be. Nothing escapes me, no dead angles, no dead space. I heard what you and the Artist were talking about earlier, and before that, the DHR. . .'

While he's speaking you clutch at the mango you just found at your feet.

'I'm not here to pinch your fruit. You didn't object when Lully Madeira pinched everything off you just now, though, did you? You let him fill his booty bag! Relax, I won't be eating that, I've got my own; I mostly consume the idiocy of others, to make them a little wiser, get what I mean? I've come to consume your idiocy, but first you need to know a little more about me...'

He still doesn't sit down, which bothers you; you have to keep your head raised to listen.

'Allow me to introduce myself, young man... I could easily be your great-grandfather, you haven't a grey hair on your head. Round here they call me Black Mamba. I'd like you to call me that too, because I have a third eye, keener even than the eye watching Cain, the elder son of Adam and Eve, humanity's first murderer! You've been sitting at the foot of this tree for quite a while, and now you've got a mango in your hand, like some imbecile who doesn't know whether to eat it or give it to those ravenous crows peering down at you. Lost in your own ego, you fear everything, even your own shadow, which fortunately cannot be seen since we lot don't have the luxury of admiring our own reflection, not even in its deepest darkest form...'

'This mango just dropped off the tree and—'

'Did I ask you to explain? What makes you think you can interrupt an elder when he's talking? No one here opens their mouth when Black Mamba's speaking! Do that one more time and I'm leaving! Only one person round here has the right to speak, and that's me. I'm the keeper of words and I deal them out one at a time, just like Mount Nabemba in the distance there, revealing its secrets only to those who climb it in true humility. Do you get what I'm saying, little greenhorn?'

You huddle down small. He pauses for breath and continues:

'I know, I know, you think I'm just some madman, just some piece of rubbish from a bin in the Trois-Cents! Just because I'm small I bet you're thinking, *What a funny little old guy!* But the truth of the matter is, Frère-Lachaise won't welcome you with open arms like some street walker dragging her limbs along the pavements of this town! I know you still haven't accepted your death. Oh, don't worry, I haven't come to read you the riot act, and I'm certainly not going to take you somewhere to face the Last Judgement. All those stories about judgement in the world beyond are bullshit. Poppycock they fed you at Thanks Be to God, and you don't need me to remind you how things ended up there! What just *kills* us in here is the knife of conscience, the sense that our life hung by a thread that we ourselves have broken. Let me say it loud and clear: all death is deserved, even the death of a seed that never burst, or that, on bursting, lived but a single hour...'

He spits and the gob lands a short distance off; he scrapes at the earth with his right foot to cover it.

'Every inch of this place belongs to me. I was here in the beginning, am now, and ever shall be; it's me that nominates the heads of department to the elders, who must confirm my choice with a unanimous vote. I put forward Prosper Milandou since he arrived here in all humility, even though his profile would have merited a place in the rich folk's cemetery. He's a brilliant man, a discerning man; when he visits the rich folk's cemetery with me, he even impresses the white folk lying there. He knows the history of France, he's familiar with French culture, and is therefore welcome at all the grand dinners and celebrations held at the cemetery, where he is listened to and applauded, while I glow with pride like Artabanus, Prince of Persia, basking in reflected glory. The greatest sign of intelligence is to recognise intelligence in others. And Prosper Milandou, humble as he is, accepted my authority. He never interrupted me when I was speaking, not like you newbies. Anyway, how come you turn up on my patch without coming to say hello?'

'I don't know anyone, I don't know where your grave is!'

He looks up at the sky. Three crows hover over your head. Probably the same ones waiting to pounce on your mango earlier, back checking if you've hopped off and left your piece of fruit behind.

'I've been dead for half a century now, with only my own folly to blame. You and I are the same like that, victims of our own stupidity. I don't know how to explain it to you. I'll try, and please don't interrupt me because I swear if you do I will get up and leave and you'll hear nothing more. I'll do my utmost to ensure your death is a bed of nails, do you hear me? I can't bear being interrupted...'

After a few seconds' silence he is visibly reassured, clears his throat and begins:

'In my lifetime, I was Black Mamba, the keeper of Frère-Lachaise. I worked all day and all night, I was like part of the furniture around here, and for many people Frère-Lachaise was synonymous with Black Mamba, the very same one you see before you now! In reality, people scarcely saw me, as though I came from another time. The cabin at the entrance to the cemetery was my second home. I called it, affectionately, "my office". Inside those thirty square metres I had my gas stove, a little fridge, a few pots, a stool, a folding bed and a little table. Some of these were given to me by bereaved families in recognition of my kindness to them, accompanying them to the tomb of their loved one, even though I didn't have to. I ate and I slept there. The only holiday I took each year was 15 August, the national anniversary of Independence. Unsurprisingly, as the government didn't allow burials to take place that day I was free to party too, to blend with the crowd, to dance, to get drunk, as Pontenegrins do on that special day. Rings a bell, does it, 15 August? Isn't that why you're here now? No need to answer, I know it's a fateful date for you! Well anyway, I'll leave that to your conscience too, make up your own mind, ask yourself how you want things to be, now your life is over, and you have your whole death in front of you to reflect... So this cabin became both my home and my office, but 15 August was the one day of the year I always spent elsewhere. I could go back into town, to my home, have a nice shower to get rid of the smell of the dead – oh yes, the dead smell really bad, don't let's bury our heads in the sand – sit at a proper dining table, help myself to a nice dish of plantains with pork, sleep in a comfortable bed and have sweet dreams about something other than Frère-Lachaise. As for the house in the Roy Quarter, I inherited it when my father died, three years after my mother. They both died of the same illness, cholangiocarcinoma, otherwise known as bile-duct cancer, a rare kind of tumour according to the doctors, but which, as though by a stroke of fate, struck our family twice over. My little sister – there was only two years between us – had followed her Angolan husband, a rebel under the insurgent leader Jonas Savimbi, who was constantly threatening the government in power. I would never hear again from this sister – even the day our father died she didn't show up, though I had the body held at the morgue for fifteen days in the hope she might. To this day I have no idea what became of her, if she's still alive and living in Angola, or if the government in power killed her along with her husband. The family home passed into my hands, I could sell it if I wanted. The plot was fenced off with barbed wire, to discourage passers-by from cutting across the yard to get to the street behind without even saying hello. They would rather cut themselves lifting up the barbed wire than just walk round the house. When my father died I removed this protection and curiously far fewer people entered, as though they only did it before to annoy my parents and show them it doesn't do to be selfish in this world, that the earth belongs to us all...'

He spits again, this time between his legs, and steps on it with his right foot. His tattered clothing flutters in the wind. . .

'Yes, when I was alive I worked as a warden in this cemetery. My work tools? A hoe, to take out the weeds between gravestones, a rake to gather them up, a wheelbarrow to take them to a pile in a corner of the burial ground, to burn them once they'd been dried by the sun. I also had a torch so I could find my way around at night if I heard something unusual close by. It was only animals from outside coming into the plot, probably because the bins of Pointe-Noire had run out of things for them to get their teeth into. I saw so many cats with bristling fur. Not to mention the dogs with spiralled tails, or chickens laying misshapen eggs under bushes. I would come across all kinds of hideous beasts: black snakes, long and glistening, slithering into tombs through openings I blocked up the next day; rats scurrying about, avoiding the light of my torch; lizards, inflating their scarlet crests when disturbed, and all manner of other things. My machete was my weapon of defence. At first I asked for a firearm, but sadly the town hall made it clear that my profession was not considered sufficiently dangerous for me to be issued with this means of protection. I was a bit cross about this – what did a bunch of bureaucrats from the town hall know? They just made money from the dead, I was the one putting my life at risk whenever bandits broke in and got up to no good! Also the way the bureaucrats managed the space made me really wonder what sort of world we live in! Their job was to organise things properly, according to the requirements of the law. In developed countries things are done properly: the council has the land surveyed to establish the capacity of the cemetery and to separate private and common land, all in accordance with the population of the city, the number of deaths, the level of demand. But here it's chaos, the way the dead get buried on top of the dead; they bring in corpses from far and wide, when to qualify for burial here you have to live in the commune of Pointe-Noire, or at least own a private piece of land in the cemetery. And all those guys at the town hall treated me like shit, like owl turd! Whenever they were short of staff I had to drop my warden activity and help the funeral workers with planning or the undertakers with digging! Does that seem normal to you? So, as my whole life was based at Frère-Lachaise, this was where I brought the little chicks I picked up in the rough districts. The poor girls were terrified when I made a date with them at the cemetery, but if I explained my job calmly they understood in the end and decided I wasn't a sexual pervert, a necrophile. Even so, they'd turn up trembling, and sometimes it was hard for me to really enjoy myself; the slightest noise terrified them, made them tense up, and after that the only thing you could do was listen to the radio playing folk music from Central Africa till break of day, when they'd leave, making it clear that if I wanted to see them again I must get a hotel room or take them back to my place...'

A plane crosses the sky. As it vanishes over the horizon, you follow it with your gaze.

But Black Mamba will not be distracted from his tale.

'My work was well paid, I had no complaints; nights were paid double and I had a kind of security since I wasn't concerned that someone would come and pinch my job. No one was shoving their way through the door to come and watch over the sleep of the dead. In fifteen years of work I had never been worried or troubled by the slightest incident, till the cursed day my excessive tolerance caused me to make a slip. The first few years I was quite bored, it felt like a bit of a sinecure. I killed time between the arrival of remains by reading. I read a bit of everything: comics, detective novels I bought outside the Rex cinema. Hang on, though, I never said I *only* read detective novels! I particularly loved romantic novels by

Guy des Cars; he was so good at telling love stories, you let yourself be taken in. But there was one book I loved most of all...'

He fumbles inside his ragged clothing and brings out the book he had in his hands when he arrived at your grave. The title is scarcely legible, the pages are yellowed, the back cover has been torn off.

'Yes, it's this one! *The Jerusalem Bible!* There's everything in this book: the beginning, the end, the past, the future, good, evil, angels, devils, earth, sky, sea, fire, everything, including nothingness! It's quite possible I was – in fact I'm sure I was – the only person in the whole country who read this book every year, from cover to cover; all those Christians out there pretend to have read it but it's not true. And I always found new things, as though each time an invisible hand had added new truths, to enlighten me further! I also had a Brandt radio with four wavelengths, which was useful for listening to the announcement of deaths, so I'd know ahead of time who was going to turn up for burial at Frère-Lachaise. I wrote down the name of the deceased person and kept an eye out for them from my cabin. When I saw a funeral procession arriving I could always tell who it was. And as soon as they had been buried, I would cross out their names in my arrivals book. If I'd heard a corpse mentioned on the radio but they weren't brought into the cemetery, I knew they must be being buried somewhere else: in the little cemetery in Voungou, at Matolo, in the Mongo cemetery or even, for the happy few who had lived a life of luxury, in the rich folk's cemetery. When I took my daily rest, between one and two p.m., I got my cousin to replace me, though it scared him stiff. I was preparing him to take over from me one day, but his parents were opposed to the idea, because the young man started talking to himself and at night was haunted by ghosts strangling him. You'd see him walking the city streets barefoot and bare-chested. I explained to the family it wasn't the work that had driven him mad; there were already two madmen on his father's side, it was quite probably hereditary or some kind of curse, and the parents needed to hold a family meeting and sort it out. At this they all ganged up on me. They accused me of putting a spell on my own parents in order to inherit the family house. I mean honestly, did I need a family house? So I became increasingly isolated, no one talked to me, on either my mother or my father's side. The two camps were unanimous in their judgement: to be caretaker of a cemetery you had to be a sorcerer. Therefore, whenever and wherever someone died, it was me that did it; I'd clearly put a spell on them to get their corpse into Frère-Lachaise and do things to them that modesty prevents me from going into the details of here, but which I expect you can well imagine. The worst of it was, my maternal and paternal families spread rumours about me, the craziest being that Frère-Lachaise cemetery paid me on commission. Meaning that the more corpses I brought in, the more I got paid, and when there weren't enough, I had to make arrangements to get some. So to reach my target, I was supposedly attacking my own family! You're young, Liwa, and have no grey beard – can you believe in such things? Do people accuse the midwives at Adolphe-Cissé hospital of being paid by the number of births, and of going round looking for some if there aren't enough? You see my problem, little Liwa Ekimakingaï!'

He draws breath for a moment, then expels it from his thorax, continuing:

'After that an elderly relative on my father's side turned up from the village to preach at me and tell me to stop "eating" members of our family, because a distant cousin only eight years old had died and a person shouldn't die at that age. I thought I must be dreaming! I had never met this girl in my life, and I was suddenly being accused of causing her death by magic intervention! I wouldn't even know how to set about eating someone! The old man insisted that the village

139

sorcerers, who see everything that happens at night, were unanimous: I was the culprit. They had seen the image of my face appear in a bowl. I had no idea what he meant, so the old man explained that the practice of the bowl involved filling a dish with water and asking the spirits to make the face of the wrongdoer appear on the surface once the water settles. And according to this old guy, mine were the features revealed, several times over! I told him to take a hike, find his idiot sorcerers a decent ophthalmologist. The old man got angry, insulted me, pulled down his pants to show me his sagging butt, the most terrible curse he could have laid on me. I just said to myself, oh well, I don't need these people to get on with my life. I severed all my links with them and continued with my solitary existence, focussing my energies on my career.'

His bottom lip trembles nervously. Two vertical lines run down his face. He retreats inside himself, in a way you've never seen before:

'You need to know everything about me, Liwa. In a cemetery there are as many stories as there are graves. . . I'll spare you the details of my family squabbles. The point is, I went on with my job, and I began to love my profession as caretaker at Frère-Lachaise. Years went by, and my reputation for eating people reached the town of Pointe-Noire. People were frightened when I passed them in the street. Then one day, as I was quietly reading my Bible in my cabin, I saw a man and a woman engaged in the sexual act on one of the graves in the middle of the cemetery, right there. . .'

He points to a place behind you and you turn.

'That's right, there in the middle. That's where it happened! The couple were humping like rabbits on the tomb of old Mâ Mapassa's twins, and those two poor children had done nothing to deserve such an act of profanity. At first I said to myself that the man and woman were creatures from the other world, so I shouldn't be surprised to find them making out on a gravestone. I went on browsing in my Bible, but something told me this was the first time I had seen them at Frère-Lachaise and that they were quite the opposite of deceased. I can tell the wheat from the chaff, the living from the dead; I pretty well knew the faces of all my lot, I had seen them arrive, and most of those who had come before me had been moved to the rich folk's cemetery when we almost had a riot in the town, when the middle classes started to say they didn't want their dead to be buried along with the dead from the poorer districts. I won't go back over all that; Prosper Milandou has already told you the story, and given a flawless recital of the letter His Excellency Théophile-Florent Tsiba de Montaigne wrote to President Papa Mokonzi Ayé alias Zarathustra to recommend he get involved in the affair. . .'

He stops and looks pointedly at you, as though waiting for you to agree that Prosper Milandou did indeed speak of these things. When you nod in acknowledgement he is overjoyed:

'Well, there you go! So, I didn't recognise this couple doing indecent things at Frère-Lachaise, I'd never seen them before, and I came out of my cabin with a machete in my hand, to go over to the twins' tomb. At this point the man and woman started dressing again in haste, and made to run off. But which way would they go, since the entrance was behind me? The concession was enclosed in long, high walls; you'd need wings to get out. Realising they could not escape the situation, they fell to their knees, in a sign of submission. I came up close, my machete raised above my head. The man told me that a sorcerer had given them instructions for his sterile wife to get pregnant. They must find a tomb of a pair of twins and have sex on it. The wife, who kept her head bowed, raised it to add that they'd been trying unsuccessfully to have a child for the last ten years, European medicine had been unable to help with their misfortune. What would you have done in my shoes, Liwa? Denounce them to the police for profaning a grave? I took pity on them, and told them to scarper. But instead of getting to their feet they stayed kneeling.

'Get out!' I yelled, threatening them with my machete. No reaction. They did not move, and showed no intention of clearing off. The man murmured that actually he had not had time to ejaculate, that I had interrupted him just as he was about to come! He started sniffling, begging me to give them just fifteen minutes more. This was their last chance, whined his wife. If they didn't get the deed done, she would have no reason to carry on living in this cruel world, where sterile women were regarded as she-devils. I was in a real fix, I don't mind telling you, Liwa. If one of the council bosses arrived and saw, I would be fired without compensation. On the other hand, the woman's distress was breaking my heart. In the end I cracked, and that's where I made the worst mistake of my life. The man and woman went back to the twins' gravestone. I did not move from my spot. I saw them undress and get back down to business. The man, instead of concentrating on what he was doing, was looking over at me. Conscious that disturbing them might well make him dry up, I left the cemetery to have a smoke, till the couple passed me on the way out, thanking me and getting into a car parked several hundred metres from the entrance to the cemetery, to drive back into town. . .'

His eyes are damp, his voice trembles. You feel remorse weighing down on him and his confession, which you cannot bear to interrupt, seems like an important moment for him, a kind of inner liberation. You feel rather sorry for him, imagining how often he must have said all this, re-reading in the library of his memory these scenes which must surely be written in indelible ink.

He breaks in on your reverie:
'Are you still with me?'

142

You hesitate to answer, since he's told you not to disturb him in his tale. He's pleased you've understood this, and now he's setting off again like a car that ran out of petrol for a moment and has now refuelled again:

'Three years had passed since the incident with the couple. My life at Frère-Lachaise was incredibly calm, till the day I had a visit from a couple. I thought they had come to visit the future resting place of their lost loved one, before the burial the following day. But no, it was the same couple I had disturbed on the grave of Mâ Mapassa's twins three years before. My heart skipped a beat as I emerged from my cabin: beside the couple walked two children. A boy and a girl, both dressed in white, as alike as two peas in a pod. The little girl was holding her father's hand, the little boy his mother's. I couldn't believe my eyes: so the woman had fallen pregnant and given birth to twins! I offered my congratulations, and the couple seemed joyful, radiantly happy. I leaned down towards the children to say some kindly words to them. The little girl looked at me so intensely, it gave me quite a shock. Trying to avoid her piercing gaze, I turned to the boy and held out my hand. He took it and lowered his eyes. His hand was so cold, it felt like squeezing an ice cube. The parents tried to encourage them to be nice to me, but the children seemed in a hurry to leave. A quarter of an hour later, escorting the little group back to the main entrance, I saw the parents' car parked a bit further down, on the same spot as three years earlier. I stood outside the cemetery as the family left. The car nosed its way slowly onto the avenue, heading into town. Back in my cabin I found it hard to shake off the memory of the little girl's intense gaze, and the feeling of the little boy's frozen hand even more so. Instinctively I opened my own hand; the mark of the child's had remained in my own. A black line in the form of a small cross.'

He shows you the palm of his right hand:

'Look, the mark is still there, even after my own death,

three days after the couple's visit. Yes, I died here, in my cabin, the day after Independence Day, after I'd been partying with some chicks from the Rex district. Returning home at dawn, I felt heavy, my right palm was burning, and the mark of the cross scratched into it was growing bolder. I was so frightened I consulted my Bible. The words in the chapters of Apocalypse were almost leaping off the page, the verses all jumbled together, and everything around began to tremble. My final image was most strange: I saw two children dressed in white, each upon a horse, holding a sharp-edged sword in their hands. Then utter darkness fell upon me, and when I awoke I felt as you must have done, as though a great tremor had ripped open the earth all around me, and I had been swept up by a cyclone and tossed over a grave which would become my own. I was by now in a different world, the one you and I are in now... Since then I have made my peace with Mâ Mapassa's twins; I take great care of their grave, I treat their mother most respectfully whenever she comes to lay flowers where they rest. Liwa, are you asleep?'

He's right, you are. Black Mamba scrutinises you, leans over and sniffs at you, before heading off towards the exit. When you re-open your eyes it's too late: he has gone from your graveside. The dust sweeps up the dead leaves, and once everything grows calm you look over in the direction Black Mamba could have gone, but there's no sign of him anywhere; it's as if he never passed this way, as if he never told you his tale...

Crow Woman

———

YOU HADN'T NOTICED HER till now: the whole sky has darkened, the day has gone to break elsewhere, in some part of the world far away from Frère-Lachaise.

But before nightfall, you had one final visitor, Liliane Bilongo, known as 'Crow Woman', whose legend, she claimed, had crossed the Congo borders, reaching as far as Angola and Gabon.

You were deeply touched by her story. Perhaps also because the woman's face was burned away, her nose almost entirely gone. The nasal timbre would have been unbearable without the compensating softness of her voice. When she spoke, jets of saliva shot out like projectiles, landing at your feet. Probably because she only had two teeth left in her mouth: long, pointed canines, which gave her a Dracula-like appearance.

No, she swore you had nothing to fear from her, she had never sucked the blood of those she referred to as the 'enemies of innocence'. She was in fact known for her fierce hostility towards the paedophiles of Pointe-Noire, whose genitals she would rip out with a single bite while they slept.

She had never had children, but considered all the kids of Pointe-Noire as her own, and that she had a duty to protect them. They called her Crow Woman because she dressed in black from head to toe. At the time of these battles she was around forty years old. She would transform herself into an adolescent and the enemies of innocence walked into her trap. She would enter the dreams of these individuals, where they would all see her in the guise of a siren, with long blonde hair down to the small of her back, Barbie eyes, black skin and a suggestive demeanour that worked its magic on them. Still in their dreams the men would follow her into a hotel room, sprawl on the bed while she undressed them, rocking them, till they woke with a start, screaming for help at the top of their voices. Too late: they lay in a pool of blood, their sex ripped off with such violence it must have been the act of some wild beast, mad with hunger, produced by their nightmare.

When word got round that it was Liliane Bilongo – the sterile woman, who had no descendants and whose lineage was shrouded in mystery – who had entered the dreams of these men and bitten off their sex, the authorities joined forces against her and accused her of 'witchcraft conducted in broad daylight, with antediluvian techniques'. The speedy reaction of the politicians arose not from their concern for the common good: several of the individuals guilty of these crimes occupied high positions in the civil service. These distinguished citizens, with their connections, obtained Crow Woman's arrest for 'heresy', and demanded she suffer the same penalty as that eighteenth-century Angolan female known as Kimpa Vita.

Few Pontenegrins, including Liliane Bilongo's detractors, grasped the implications of the comparison with Kimpa Vita. At school the story of the prophetess of the Kongo kingdom who fought for the unification of her native land was never taught. In fact she had created her own religious movement, avoiding what was preached by the white missionaries like the plague. It was not to last: King Pedro IV, jealous of the success of this local variant with the natives, had Kimpa Vita arrested for heresy. She was burned to death at the stake, after confessing her sins, calling God Almighty himself as her witness, though He did not intervene to deflect this appalling punishment. Though the spirit of Kimpa Vita's movement did survive among the oldest inhabitants of the kingdom of the Kongo, the white missionaries later ensured that it was stamped out. But the movement rose again, in other forms, with other prophets, who carried the torch for the woman who by now had become a heroine – Kimpa Vita.

The Crow Woman had similarly been burned alive at the Tata-Louboko stadium. She had no followers. She had no religious movement. She left for the world beyond, a Good Samaritan, who sadly had the reputation, in popular memory, of having been a sorceress who took men back to hotel rooms to murder them in the most savage manner. Because, it was said in order to hide the truth, she bore a grudge against the male sex, which had failed to provide her with an heir...

As Liliane Bilongo walked away from the grave, vanishing, like the other characters before her, in that now-familiar cloud of dust, you heard her murmur:

'If I were in your shoes, young man, I would not be going back to town to seek revenge. The noblest thing you could do would be to return to the land of the living and perform an act establishing your greatness for all eternity, breathing life and love into those from whom it has unjustly been withheld...'

AT THE CEREMONIAL

———

The Invisible Man

—

NIGHT HAS FALLEN AT FRÈRE-LACHAISE.

It feels as though you are now the only presence left after the parade of earlier on.

How long did the whole thing last? No idea. Perhaps you'll never know, but it doesn't matter anyway. It's up to you now to steer the direction of your life, or rather your death.

You tighten your bow tie. You check that the musketeer cuffs of your shirt are showing at the ends of your jacket sleeves. You turn up your three-button collar and make sure that your violet flares aren't covering up your shiny red Salamanders, so your white laces are plain to see.

The truth is you're past caring if some people find your outfit ridiculous. It's not what you wear, it's how you wear it, you tell yourself.

While you are sorting yourself out, you imagine that somewhere in the darkness, the other deceased of Frère-Lachaise are spying on your movements, saying to themselves that they knew all along you'd go back for revenge. You can almost hear Black Mamba quoting to them the proverb he claims, baselessly, originates with his tribe:

'Only a fool measures the depth of the water with both feet.'

You're not a fool, you tell yourself, you know what you're doing, and if the depth of the water needs to be measured with both feet, that's what you'll do, there's no way anyone is going to stop you. . .

You turn towards the exit.

You pass by the cabin assigned to the caretaker of Frère-Lachaise, and remember it's the one Black Mamba told you about. It's round, solidly built. The corrugated iron roof must recently have been changed; it gleams in the night as though lit by some invisible moon you hadn't noticed. So narrow is the gate of the cabin, you have to twist sideways to enter, and the window is fairly wide, protected by a rolling metal curtain, raised halfway.

Curious, you lean in to see who's inside.

All you can make out is the dim light of a candle coming from the back of the room.

There's no one there, you think to yourself, and off you set on your way once more. In fact if you had taken a moment to lean forward properly, to press your nose up against the grille on the window, which looks like one of those kiosks in a public building in Pointe-Noire, you would have seen, in the corner of the cabin, by a metal table on which three faded flowers are laid, a pudgy individual wedged into a wicker chair, chin to chest, eyes wide open, staring you in the face.

You don't know him, you haven't met before. He knows you, though; he saw you enter Frère-Lachaise amid great pomp, and seems astonished to see you doing a moonlight flit today. He watched your burial ceremony from start to finish. It was he who pressed the button from his cabin to open the cemetery gate. Then he raised the security grille of his window, before coming out to show the hearse the place that had been prepared for you. There were people everywhere yesterday, which had annoyed him rather. He was impatient for it to end, for calm to be restored. But it was also his job to be there, to supervise. So he positioned himself just behind the guys who'd carried you and placed your coffin next to the pit. He was particularly moved by the old lady yelling that she wanted to be buried with you. This was Mâ Lembé, the inconsolable, the love of your life. The singing-dancing-weeping women and her colleagues from the Grand Marché held her back, explaining that it was au revoir but not goodbye, that you were going on ahead to build a great palace in Paradise, and that when she got to the other side herself she would want for nothing.

The caretaker of Frère-Lachaise carefully watched the gestures of the four grave-attendants as they lowered your coffin into the hole using thick white ropes. Similarly, when they picked up their spades to cover you with earth. At that moment the weeping increased tenfold, as the reality of your final departure dawned on those present. Mâ Lembé had managed to escape from the group of women to get within a few centimetres of the hole in the ground, and had been caught by the grave-attendants just as she was about to jump in, before you'd even been lowered down yourself.

The prayers and funeral orations went on and on, as though they were trying to defer the fatal moment. The caretaker had got through an entire packet of cigarettes, leaving the stubs scattered at his feet.

The hour had come, the spadefuls of earth landed on your coffin with a sound that was both loud and muffled, till the point when nothing more was heard and the crowd stood looking at a small mound with a wooden cross planted on the top. The caretaker walked back to his cabin, and as he did so said to himself under his breath, shaking his head in disbelief:

'That young man won't stay with us more than forty-eight hours, I can tell; he'll never accept his death. . .'

You come across a long stick placed to one side, just outside the main gate. You don't think it's a tool left behind by the undertakers, much more likely the weapon used by the caretaker of Frère-Lachaise to protect himself at night from spirits, or from the living who climb in over the wall to steal the precious items that the families of the deceased bury with their loved ones. You turn around to check that the caretaker isn't behind you, then seize hold of the weapon, taking great care not to touch the two-sided blade that gleams even in the black of night.

The gate opens. Probably the caretaker, controlling it from his lodge. He understands he cannot oppose your will.

You march resolutely out of the graveyard and the gate swings shut behind you with the loud creak of an ancient machine that hasn't been oiled for a good long time.

You observe the lights down below; the town is evidently popping and you decide to make your way there, keeping a tight hold of the shaft of your spear, with the blade pointing downwards. . .

Memories of the Ceremonial

———

YOU'RE WALKING ALONG THE EDGE of the rue du Repos, the only tarmacked road that leads from Frère-Lachaise into town. It's the road the procession took when they brought you yesterday.

You can hear the tread of your Salamanders on the bitumen. Occasionally you stop and turn around to see how far you've come, then set off on your way again, aware that just because you can see light on the horizon doesn't mean the city's close by. It's almost as though the more you focus your gaze on it, the further you seem to have to go. So you continue to walk in the familiar twilight, your gaze fixed on the surface of the road.

A vehicle approaches, its headlights bearing down on you. You conceal the spear behind your back, you freeze, you close your eyes. It draws level with you, the driver leans on his horn and you hear a shout of laughter, as though he's making fun of you. It's probably your outfit, you think, before setting off again, allowing your thoughts to turn to that Saturday, 15 August, when everything happened, no more than five days ago.

You recall the fever of excitement you felt that day, along with the rest of the population, for 15 August is a day when everyone goes wild with joy. The celebration of Independence. You'd decided to spend the evening at the Ceremonial.

It was two years since you had last visited the discotheque. And yet your memories of it were not unpleasant. So when slanderers said it had become a temple of depravity, luring souls from the path of righteousness, you dismissed them with a wave of the hand. The girls who hung out at the Ceremonial were brazen harlots, they said; anyone who wanted could take them back home for a glass of Primus. Jehovah's Witnesses preaching at the city roundabouts called the place Sodom or Gomorrah and swore with their right hand on the Bible that just like those cities of long-ago Canaan, the Ceremonial would one day be cataclysmically destroyed, as a sign of God's punishment for the wicked.

You didn't really get this belief, which seemed to be held mostly by people who had never set foot in the place. Personally, you'd been pretty satisfied with your experience of two years before, and had not forgotten it. Back then, you recall as though it was yesterday, you picked up one of the young ladies normally propped up at the bar with free drinks for the whole evening, and it hadn't cost you a fortune, if you discounted the one drink you bought her to strike up a conversation and the cost of the hotel room at Life and a Half. You couldn't ask her back to your place, Mâ Lembé would have asked questions, and in any case, you weren't going to embark on a night of funny business in the room next door to your grandmother's. You'd never done that before, in fact Mâ Lembé had always wondered if you weren't actually still a sexual innocent. She had no idea that when you wanted to have a good time you took a room in one of the hotels in the Trois-Cents, or the Rex district. A far cry from when you and your partners in crime, José and Sosthène, hid in half-built or abandoned houses to discover the secrets of sexuality for which no adult had supplied a map. You read magazines for over-eighteens from the kiosk outside the Rex picture house and admired the posters of naked white women – magazines with black women didn't exist – fantasized over their incomparable breasts, the perfect compass-drawn circle of their backsides, till the day you cracked and decided to cross the Rubicon of these sterile projections. You too, in other words, would go to the Rex district, where the prostitutes known to Pontenegrins as 'Zaire mamas', who had taught many young people of Pointe-Noire the secrets of the female body, would help you take the plunge with a naked girl ...

So there you were in the hotel room at Life and a Half, with this girl telling you to get a move on:

'Let's get on with it, then, I have to get home; my son's waiting for me, he needs a feed at six in the morning...'

You were caught short and didn't know what to do. But the girl helped you undress, and from there it all went so fast you didn't know what was going on: you found yourself alone at first light, and the only sign of what had taken place was the condom by the bed.

You returned to the Ceremonial the next weekend, hoping to see the girl again, or find a different one to take to the Life and a Half. Your young lady wasn't there, just women of a certain age discussing their widowhood, separations, divorces. They all hoped to shack up as quickly as possible with the first barn rooster to show. As soon as a young man came down the stairs and stepped into the basement where the dance floor was, these desperate women got out their claws and pounced brazenly upon their prey.

That wasn't what you wanted. Besides, you preferred not to think about the other time, just before the girl with the long legs, when, for want of a better offer, you'd had to make do with a nervous and manic widow. She had followed you round the entire evening, showing her claws as soon as another, younger woman came near you. You were 'her young man of the evening'. It was her idea to go back to her place, though you'd booked a room as usual at the Life and a Half. Once you got to her home, though, there was sadly nothing doing. The woman tensed up, saying her deceased husband was watching you do your filthy business, it was putting her off. First of all she had to apologise to him, explaining to her dear departed that time had passed, she had the right to life after him, and that being dead didn't give him the right to be angry with the whole world.

The widow spent the entire rest of the night telling you about her deceased husband, an ex-station master on the railways, who died after a work accident. She told you the story of the funeral, to the last detail. The widow explained she'd had difficulty getting the inheritance she'd hoped for; she'd been disinherited overnight by her brothers-in-law who had pounced with indecent haste on the possessions of the deceased, down to his dirty underwear, holey socks and worn-out toothbrushes. You learned that the ex-railwayman had been buried in a zinc coffin, dressed all in red, not at Frère Lachaise but at the Cemetery of the Rich.

At any rate, it was probably this last encounter with the widow that made you decide to draw a line under your visits to the Ceremonial. You had been upset, too, by the behaviour of the young girl with long legs, who had vanished from circulation, as though your meeting had been just a brief interlude, an error on her part, when you thought it might have been possible to work things out.

You shut yourself away. You'd go to work, go back home, have a chat with your grandmother, have something to eat, then go to bed. This was the kind of routine Mâ Lembé approved of; at last you were showing some common sense. If you went out at all, you stayed close to the house, often walking down the avenue de l'Indépendence or the rue du

Joli-Soir, where you'd buy some Benin mash and mood balls. Maybe because you worked as a commis de cuisine you avoided so much as putting a pot on the stove at home, in case it reminded you of work, an activity you were intent on forgetting the second you hung up your apron and cap in the cloakroom at the Victory Palace hotel. Nor did you want to force Mâ Lembé to cook regularly, even though she still often did. Usually you would bring food home from work in little plastic boxes, having dodged the watchful eye of your chef, Monsieur Montoir. Mâ Lembé really enjoyed this, and would eat a little of everything, though she'd push away the camembert:

'It's gone off,' she'd say. 'If you ask me, the whites didn't want it; they threw it away and you got it back out of the bin!'

She loved the red wine:

'Now that really is delicious, not all mouldy like the cheese...'

You'd laugh at all this. You'd look across at her, dozing at the table, and you knew the years were galloping now, but that this woman had risen above time itself, as she was inclined to say:

'Some days I feel like death is ashamed of me. It walks past me in the street, it looks at me, then runs off to tap on someone else's shoulder. But it did take Albertine from me, and I'll never forgive it for that!'

She'd lean on the edge of the table to stand up and disappear into her bedroom, and fifteen minutes later you'd hear her snoring away...

The Mananas Salesman

———

ON THE EVENING OF INDEPENDENCE DAY you decided to pick up where you had left off at the Ceremonial. The club would be packed. It was every year on 15 August. Even those who never normally went out dressed up to the nines, almost as though people were just waiting for this day. All year long they complained they were broke and suddenly there they were on Independence Day shelling out vast sums, buying whole cases of Primus or imported beer.

You got ready with great care.

After your shift, around four in the afternoon, you took a bus to the Grand Marché, to visit Abdoulaye Walaye, your outfitter, as you liked to call him, one of the few shopkeepers in town you had confidence in. It was he who recommended the shirt with the round musketeer cuffs and a three-button collar, the flared violet trousers and the polished red Salamander shoes with white laces.

Abdoulaye Walaye convinced you that these clothes and these shoes basically had your name on them, that he was selling them specially for Independence Day, and the heads of the whole town would turn as you passed, especially the women's.

You liked the sound of this, and forgot that Abdoulaye Walaye was first and foremost a salesman like all the rest, and his main concern was to get rid of his merchandise as fast as possible. What did he care if the sleeves of your jacket hardly reached your wrists, or your trousers were a bit short for a man of your height?

'Do you not have a more comfortable size?' you wondered, swaddled in the suit he'd told you to try.

As though anticipating this reaction he replied:

'Comrade, this is how to dress! Take a look at yourself in the mirror; you're looking good, no? Like a Prime Minister! Look at those shoulders! You're the lucky one, comrade!'

'What about the sleeves? I just feel like the jacket's a bit—'

'What sleeves? What jacket? It's all good, take my word for it!'

'Really?'

'I dress the mayor, the prefect, doctors, every civil servant in town! That's what they're all wearing! The sleeves of the jacket are short to allow the shirt sleeves to show a little, it's a sign of elegance! Like in Paris!'

Abdoulaye Walaye folded up the clothes and put them in a bag, as though it was already a done deal.

He usually won at this game. He'd name a price and wrap up the goods before the customer even had time to respond.

'I'm selling at a loss, comrade!'

You paid and you left the shop, still feeling quite uncertain. At home you tried several times to stretch the material of the jacket; you felt the sleeves of a shirt should never under any circumstances show at the cuffs of the jacket.

In the end you decided you didn't look ridiculous, after all; the mayor, the prefect, the doctors and the civil servants all dressed like this too. . .

*

At six o'clock, showered and dressed, you were once more assailed with doubt. You managed to overcome it: you did a few fancy steps in front of the mirror, moving it to show your reflection at a more flattering angle.

By the end you felt there was nothing really wrong, the suit actually looked good on you. You didn't look as ridiculous as you had feared. You were proud of your height, and sensed that women were more attracted to tall men; no one noticed the little guys. You'd have been ridiculous if you'd been small, you say to yourself. You'd have drowned in these clothes...

You had meant to go out around ten in the evening but you were ready by half seven and bursting with impatience! You just couldn't wait. You needed something to do. You decided to go out and break in the leather on your new shoes, get a sense of how people felt about your outfit.

An old man turned round, raised his hat and bowed to you.

A hundred metres further on, a young girl overtook you and ignored you, hurrying to the bus stop at the Vicky Photo Studio on the avenue de l'Indépendence.

A bit further down, at the crossing of the rue Kimangou-Roger and the avenue des Trois-Martyrs you met two young people who burst out laughing when they saw you.

You stopped, furious:

'You laughing at me?'

'We didn't even notice you,' one of them retorted.

You beat a retreat and made your way down the rue des Martyrs as far as Hamza's bazaar, where the Lebanese shopkeeper ran an expert eye over you and said:

'There's something missing, comrade...'

'Really? What?' you said in surprise, staring hard at the sleeves of your jacket.

'Think about it!' answered Hamza, touching the tip of his nose.

'I don't see...'

'When you're all dressed up like that, what's the other thing you need, comrade?' Hamza wandered off to the back of the shop. He took a ladder, climbed up three steps, picked out a bottle and blew the dust off it.

He came back to you, smiling from ear to ear:

'This is what you need, Mananas eau de toilette! Women love it, believe me!'

'Is that the only one you have?'

'Why? Have you got a problem with Mananas?'

'Well, it's what they use to cover the smell of dead bodies. . .'

'Who told you that nonsense? That's rubbish, comrade! I swear, it's how I hooked my wife twenty years back in Beirut! Folk talk nonsense. Use that and I guarantee you'll be back with good news tomorrow!'

You went back home with your eau de toilette, not intending to use it. But at half past nine in the evening, while you were combing your hair one final time, you spotted the Mananas you'd left lying on the bed. You opened it and applied it lavishly till the whole bottle was almost empty, then turned off the storm lamp and set off again down the rue des Martyrs. . .

Dance Partner of 15 August

———

IT WAS TRICKY FINDING TRANSPORT because of the holiday, but you managed to catch a taxi that had stopped just in front of you, maybe, you thought, because you'd scrubbed up well, compared to other Pontenegrins. The taxi driver even suggested as much:

'Why, young man, you're dressed like a real prince.'

No one had ever paid you a compliment before. He set off like a shot down the streets parallel to the avenue de l'Indépendence, avoiding the traffic jams. . .

The taxi dropped you outside the Ceremonial thirty minutes later. One thing was really different: you had to ring several times, wait for them to open the door after they'd inspected you through a spyhole, then pay to get in, whereas two years earlier entrance had been free.

The door opened and a security guard, silent as a sphinx, gave you a body search and sniffed before telling you with a nod to go down to the basement, which was already throbbing with sound.

*

Yes, the Ceremonial had really changed in the past year. Huge mirrors had been placed round the edges of the space. You could watch yourself dance and, better still, covertly watch the movements and gestures of the female dancers. Red velvet seating ran along the walls. The dance floor had been enlarged a bit and cemented; gone were the days when you'd come out of the discotheque to find your shoes covered in dust.

The light was too dim for your taste, you could hardly make out the people boogieing on the dance floor. Couples were grooving, entwined, to the rhythm of sixties rumba. They were playing a song by Wendo Kolosoy, 'Independence Cha-cha-cha'. How were you going to make your way through to your favourite spot on the other side, with a view of the whole dance floor?

You stopped off at the bar, ordered a glass of rum and handed the barman a 500 CFA franc note just as Wendo Kolosoy's song was coming to an end, segueing into Franco Luambo Makiadi's 'Freedom'.

The dance floor was bustling, as always when the music changed. Under cover of the shake-up you cut your way through the crowd, glass in hand, jostling a few tipsy dancers, treading on some toes.

You finally reached your favourite spot, and stood propped up against one of the two doorposts by the ladies' toilets. That was the place to stand if you were smart and didn't want to dance much, aiming at a discreet approach to the women entering or exiting the toilets.

You took a gulp of rum and examined each face as best you could. There was no one you knew; the Ceremonial drew a younger crowd these days. The women of a certain age, separated, divorced or widowed, must have abandoned the venue, probably because of the competition from hot young things in short skirts, suggestively displaying their assets.

You were about to knock back the rest of your drink, when someone tapped you on the shoulder:

'You're blocking my view! And I hate your perfume...'

It was a young girl of around twenty with her hair pulled back off her face, quite tall, wearing a body-tight dress of black lace. She was standing very straight, as though waiting for you to clear out of her line of vision at once. You stepped aside, stammering apologies which the girl didn't even bother to acknowledge. You were cross with Hamza now for recommending the disgusting eau de toilette. You felt annoyed, your pride was hurt. Maybe you should just leave, find a quieter bar on the avenue de l'Indépendence, or go eat mood balls somewhere in your own neighbourhood.

No, you would not give in. Who did this girl think she was? After all, why trust her judgement? Not every woman at the Ceremonial would agree.

After all, up to that moment no one else had said anything that unpleasant to you. You simply ignored her.

At midnight things began to take off. Champagne corks started flying, everyone cheered. On the dance floor people were singing versions of popular songs at the top of their voices, with obscene lyrics.

At the first notes of Ntesa Dalienst's hit 'Bina na ngai na respect', 'Respect me when you dance', everyone leapt onto the floor. Why should you let a comment from some random woman ruin your evening! It was time to get down and dance, so you did a circuit of the floor, looking for a possible partner.

Again, you elbowed your way through the crowd. The heat was increasing, and on a rapid inspection you failed to locate an air vent. An ancient ventilator was revolving between the two parallel doorposts at the back, where you'd positioned yourself earlier, but its worn-out blades only spread the heat generated by ecstatic bodies in hypnotic motion through the room. Unable to find a free partner, you returned to your observation post.

You'd actually identified two possible partners on the seats along the wall opposite, but shyness got the better of you. They'd probably send you packing, you and your lousy perfume! You might possibly have made a move if you were sure no one was watching and that the girl in question was alone, not with a group of friends, as many of them were, talking and laughing among themselves. A public rejection would have ruined the rest of your evening.

Back at your favourite post, you fixed your eyes on a woman sitting slightly apart from the rest, diagonally across from you. From time to time the play of lights swept across her corner, and you realised it was the young girl who had annoyed you with her remark about the smell of your eau de toilette. Even so, she was alone, 'the only lonely one', you said to yourself, with no one to get in the way, so what did you have to lose? Should you give it a shot, even if your chances of getting her to her feet were slim? How could she agree to dance with a man whose smell she couldn't stand?

Taking your courage in both hands you leapt over a pouf, then another one, and set off towards the girl, blazing your trail with a determined air, ignoring people complaining and shoving you with their elbows.

You came up to the girl and held out your arms, smiling nervously. To your great surprise she rose to her feet, straightened her dress, returned your smile and joined you on the dance floor, while most of those who had been complaining looked on enviously...

You couldn't believe you were dancing with this girl.

What about the repulsive smell of the Mananas? She'd only been kidding, she admitted, and had been surprised by your reaction. With this reassurance you could finally concentrate on the rhythm of the rumba; you needed to make a good impression to have a chance of asking her a second time. Otherwise another, bolder and more virtuosic dancer might take your place.

You avoided, at first, going 'belly to belly'. Now rumba without going belly to belly isn't a Congolese rumba, it's more the way you have to dance with your sister, aunt, mother or a family member like Mâ Lembé. In fact you wanted to show the girl you were not vulgar like the hectic groups close by, dropping their jackets, rubbing up against their partners like orangutangs in heat.

The girl herself would have none of it. After a few minutes of fumbling, eyes locked, she pulled you close to her without warning, so you were obliged to reposition, sliding your right leg between hers to let her wriggle on top of it.

Surprised, overjoyed, you yielded to the moment before telling yourself you must take matters in hand. You wrapped your long arms around the girl, then freed yourself, sending her spinning, while you took one step back, then another one forward, then made a brusque movement with your body, angling your shoulders so you could catch the girl with your right hand.

The girls sitting opposite applauded this piece of technical prowess. Your girl, delighted to have found such a supple partner, whispered in your ear that she had never danced this way before. She put her head on your right shoulder and yielded to your embrace. The dance floor was heaving, there were so many other couples and dancers; you had to hold each other ever tighter, there was so little space, and you were dancing on a patch the size of a pocket handkerchief. From then on you didn't move from the dance floor, your two bodies moving as one, while the disc jockey played one long rumba after another and the furthest thing from your mind was that this would be the final evening of your life.

The dance went on for almost an hour, and might have continued, had the disc jockey not given in to repeated pressure from two people demanding salsa. Neither you nor your partner knew how to salsa so you returned to your seats to chat. . .

You were sitting side by side.

The girl was chattier than you. You told her your name, and learned that she was Adeline, that she lived with her parents in the centre of town, towards the Côte Sauvage. The rich end, then, you thought to yourself.

And when you told her where you worked, she gave a start:

'Really? You're a cook at the Victory Palace hotel? How interesting!'

'You know it?'

'My father often eats there. . .'

'Really? What's his name?'

She didn't reply to your question, and you didn't insist.

'I have to get back. . . Will you walk me home?'

You could scarcely contain your joy; you hadn't expected this. She rose to her feet, picked up her handbag from the cloakroom, and you made for the exit, following her like a shadow.

'I'm so cold,' murmured Adeline.

You wait for a taxi to come past the Ceremonial. Not a single star was in the sky, and the wind moved in the trees all around. Yet it wasn't that cold, it was the dry season, about twenty-eight degrees.

'I'm really cold,' Adeline insisted.

Gallantly you took off your jacket and helped the young lady into it. Just then a taxi arrived.

You opened the door for her and she practically threw herself into the vehicle, while you walked round to get in the other side.

'Place Félix-Éboué,' Adeline said to the driver, and he set off without a word. She looked into your eyes now. 'What are you waiting for?'

'What do you mean, waiting?'

'Kiss me!'

The taxi driver adjusted his rear-view mirror; you could see his globular eyes rolling in lewd astonishment.

Suddenly you felt cross with yourself for being less daring, leaving the initiative to her. But you also remembered the way she had brusquely pushed your hand off her leg at the Ceremonial.

After about twenty minutes crammed into this automobile, which spluttered every fifty metres, you reached the heart of one of the swankiest parts of Pointe-Noire. Its residents called it the 'sixteenth arrondissement', referring to one of the most prestigious areas of Paris, though Pointe-Noire actually only has four arrondissements. And this sixteenth arrondissement is in fact a part of the first arrondissement, Patrice Lumumba, which is to say one of the eighty-three districts of the overall commune of Pointe-Noire. It's also the administrative and commercial centre. People who lived in the poor neighbourhoods renamed it 'MTV district', otherwise known as the 'Made to View' district. It stood in stark contrast to the poor neighbourhoods, where there was no town planning, properties were sold hand to hand and houses built overnight, encroaching on the public highway. There anyone can sell a plot belonging to anyone else, and the deed of ownership is worthless in the face of the occupier standing outside his patch of land with a machete or a rifle in his hands. Many people, for want of cash, retreated to the river banks or set up on public spaces till the authorities came to evict them, informing them that the rich wished to build a supermarket on this very spot.

In the MTV district, the territory of ex-pats, most of them European, and of the black middle classes, each home is more sumptuous than the next. Property prices ended up on a par with those in the west, the rich vying in vicious competition with each other. You had to own the most expensive house, and that had to be evident from a great distance. Lawyers, senior civil servants, ex-politicians, big businessmen, company directors – everyone knew everyone else, and they were a caste apart, and to a degree these privileged residents were strict about who they would and would not permit to move into their space. It was done by co-optation, and worked even better if you knew at least 'someone who knew someone who knew someone high up in government', as they put it, so the influential person could intervene directly with the town authorities. And when someone from this seraglio expired, the Cemetery of the Rich was close by, just overlooking the beach, less than three hundred metres from the wharf, an iron jetty used in the 1970s for the export of potassium ore found in great abundance in Tchitondi, a small neighbouring locality. Numerous people flung themselves into the sea from the wharf, causing the population to think this place must be home to evil spirits, where the undead foregathered, condemned to wander till the day some other departed folk kindly came to release them from their agony. So it was hardly surprising that feticheurs and other kinds of sorcerers from the poor neighbourhoods hung round the wharf practising their rituals, claiming to cure their clients by throwing fetishes into the sea, as well as casting spells as requested by those who came to consult them. At first light the public highway workers would go round picking up wooden hair combs, wigs, animal skulls, bottles filled with strange liquids. It wasn't just the highway workers; the police sometimes surrounded the area because a body had been fished from the water and initial investigations suggested that these were not people who had chosen to end their own lives, that there was 'something else behind it'...

*

The outer walls of the Made to View district are painted white, which brings a certain uniformity to the area. The asphalt road leading to the Côte Sauvage must be one of the best maintained in the entire city, and is dotted with ornamental trees in bloom. As the car drove along it, you were reminded, deep down, of the avenue de l'Indépendance, which runs down the middle of the Trois-Cents district. What a contrast!

A car overtook you. Yet another, coming towards you, blinded you with its headlights.

The car had stopped outside a huge plot of land, where stood an almost invisible, unlit building. For a moment you thought she must live in this strange mansion, but she turned to you and said:

'No, it's not that one, it's the third house on the right.'

Checking you were both thinking the same thing, you asked her:

'Shall I come with you?'

Her reply was both instant and laconic:

'Certainly not...'

Scarcely able to hide your disappointment, you retorted:

'So why did you bring me all the way here?'

'Help me, Liwa... Come and see me today at two o'clock.'

A car was coming up behind you.

You turned round and missed the moment when the girl ran off towards the house she'd pointed to.

As the car drew level with yours you noticed the uniform of the three people inside it. It was a private security vehicle and must have been doing a routine patrol of the district. One of the agents shone his torch on you, full in your face, then the car disappeared, turning off to the right, towards the wharf.

Adeline was no longer at the gate.

You went up to the entrance of the 'third house on the right'. You looked up at the top floor of this two-storey prosperous-looking residence, with rooftop swimming pool. It didn't seem like a good idea to hang around outside for too long, the security vehicle patrolling the district might think you were a burglar about to set to work...

You observed the light on the top floor, and even up on the roof, and the shape of a figure passing from one end to the other of the room on this level, before finally the light went out...

Now you had to take a taxi back to your own neighbourhood, and the only place to find one was by the Place Félix-Éboué, where there was more traffic, and where you'd been dropped off twenty minutes earlier.

When you finally reached the Place Félix-Éboué, you cursed: you just realised you'd forgotten to take back the jacket you'd lent Adeline when she complained of feeling cold outside the Ceremonial.

You weren't going to head back to the Côte Sauvage and shout up to her to give your jacket back. You'd get it back anyway at two o' clock, there was no hurry...

The Girl's Name

—

YOU WOKE UP AROUND MIDDAY, and told Mâ Lembé, who wanted to eat with you, that you had arranged to meet a colleague from the Victory Palace hotel at one o' clock.

Your grandmother expressed surprise:

'What's her name, Liwa, this girl you're going to see?'

Amazed at her perspicacity, you didn't answer, concentrating instead, after your shower, on what to wear.

Predictably enough, you put the same clothes back on again. You weren't going to douse yourself in Mananas, the smell was still there, more insistent than ever. And it didn't seem to bother Adeline.

At 12.45 you were waiting for a taxi on the avenue de l'Indépendence. A driver braked awkwardly alongside. You asked him to drop you by the Place Félix-Éboué, as you wanted to walk for a while too, almost a rerun of what Adeline had done a few hours earlier...

But you still had half an hour in hand. Opposite the Score supermarket you saw some kids selling flowers, and bought her a large bunch.

You wandered about, glancing at your watch every two minutes.

At 1.40 you crossed the main boulevard and finally turned into the by-now-familiar little asphalted street with its ornamental trees in bloom. A car overtook you, almost touching you, and the passengers and driver all broke into peals of laughter. No, not because of your outfit, you thought, it must be the flowers.

You looked at your watch. It was 13.59, and you stood outside the gate to the residence, which no longer felt unfamiliar.

You rang the bell and waited. . .

God's Right-hand Man

———

YOU HEARD THE STEADY TREAD OF FEET, like in a procession, approaching the door, which stood half open. You found yourself looking at a young man in military dress who was pointing a machine gun at you.

'Adeline invited me,' you stammered.

He looked you up and down, lowered his weapon then glanced at the bouquet of flowers, before barking in a military tone:

'Come in!'

A small voice whispered suddenly that you should turn back, and your heart leapt in your chest as you set eyes on a man of impressively heavy build, bald, with bulging eyes and greying temples. One metre ninety tall, he stared down at you from the vast platform of a staircase that seemed to run all the way round the house. You thought perhaps you'd got the wrong house, for the man continuing to inspect you was someone you'd already seen several times before; he was one of the most influential and feared personalities in all Pointe-Noire. You had last met only forty-eight hours before.

Yes, you'd served him at table and sometimes cooked his

meals at the Victory Palace. When the restaurant was really full and help was needed, you swapped your role as commis de cuisine for that of waiter, and were assigned several tables in the grand dining room. And you were not unhappy with the arrangement – who would not have been proud to serve an individual like Augustin Biampandou and to receive a tip that was practically equivalent to a month's pay for a waiter?

While you were struggling to keep calm and he was preparing to descend the steps to the thatched area on the right side of the yard, your thoughts returned to the eve of the festival of Independence and your visit to the Ceremonial. You harked back to the day before the great celebration because that was the day the press announced the arrival of three senior members of the Brazzaville government to celebrate with the Pontenegrins: the Minister for the Economy and Finance, Jean-Jacques Ayibaka Natongo-Tinapokoua; the Minster for Tourism, Nakoteka Mboka-Mobobi; and the Speaker of the House, Thierry Mokele-Mbemb. The parade would take place on the Place Patrice Lumumba, where the whole of Pointe-Noire would gather.

Augustin Biampandou had booked a table at the Victory Palace, in his usual spot at the back of the room, near the red velvet black-out curtains, in an intimate atmosphere which he particularly favoured. Summoned to the rescue to wait tables, you were assigned to his, and noticed the three young women sitting in a semi-circle opposite him, wearing wigs of long, golden fake hair down to their waists. When you came closer you realised they were just teenagers trying, unsuccessfully, to look grown up. At first you thought Augustin Biampandou was having lunch with his children, or even that he might be their grandfather. But the way he acted towards them: his cunning, lustful smile, the glasses of vodka being poured by the barmaid with a sullen look that conveyed her disgust at being complicit in this situation – everything confirmed that these girls, in their extremely short dresses and matching killer heels, had been invited here to indulge in activities normally reserved for adults.

Several times, your gaze collided with Augustin Biampandou's and he made it clear he didn't want you hanging around his table. You were not unaware that most people paid him respect simply so as not to invite his fury, knowing that he was liable to take extreme measures to deal with those who got in his way. Augustin Biampandou had a very shady past, and if anyone mentioned it in the media or in a private conversation that got back to him, he would make sure to 'deal with' the situation, and nothing further would be heard from the indiscreet person in days to come. So no one must ever say that he had offered up his own daughter to the ocean to gain greater influence in the city and throughout the country. It was George Moutaka, the old gardener, who told you that after the death of Samantha Biampandou, the entire police force had been mobilised in the search for the body of the girl, who was only fifteen years of age. There were two competing versions of the events leading to her death.

According to the first, Samantha had drowned in the Atlantic, close to the wharf by the Cemetery of the Rich, since she liked to bathe over there. So it was an accident, like others that had occurred in the same place, which had been cursed ever since Pontenegrins who had been captured and put onto slave-trade ships broke free and flung themselves into the water to be eaten by sharks, rather than end up as slaves on the American continent. But the sharks never ate the slaves, as though drawing attention to human atrocity. The waves, which were very rough on that coast, eventually brought the bodies up onto the beach, where they could be found laid out in rows, intact, ready for a decent burial.

But the body of Samantha Biampandou was not found in one piece: seventy-two hours after the tragedy, the waves had still only brought up individual parts of it, methodically dismembered by human hand, and not by accident, as the official police report, supported by the father himself, tried to claim. The latter declared that the affair was closed, that it was time for him to accept the death of his beloved daughter, though he stressed that he would go on mourning her till the day he died.

The second version, the one still current in popular memory, told of an act of infanticide ordered by Augustin Biampandou, who was said to have sacrificed Samantha by offering her up to the genies of the waters, so they would help him become boss of Pointe-Noire Seaport. He knew his friend, president Papa Mokonzi Ayé alias Zarathustra, would never sack his own son, who held this coveted post, with its opportunities for embezzling as much State money as you liked. He therefore had to resort to witchcraft, to soften up the President of the Republic to the point where he'd gladly topple his own son in favour of his own long-term friend. Augustin Biampandou knew that sacrifices were required on this occasion, and not animal sacrifices, as recommended by Angelou, the only woman to live with him permanently. She was not his wife, Augustin Biampandou's view was that marriage was incompatible with power, since it obliged you to share your deepest secrets with a stranger who, some day or other, would stab you in the back. Under Augustin Biampandou's roof, Angelou acted rather as 'house sorcerer', as was often the case in the homes of rich men and politicians. For decades, this woman, who had sworn to stay by his side to the very end, had been employed by Augustin Biampandou to 'see what was coming' and ward it off. And it was she who had looked after Samantha till the day she disappeared.

This time the recommendations of the house sorcerer were insufficient. Angelou was rather offended that Augustin Biampandou rejected her advice, returning instead to his town in the north, Sembé, where the ritual practices drew on those of the Wuli people from Western Cameroon. There, certain sorcerers are not living people, but the dead who

walk around inside a human form that matches any individual of their choice. The spirits of Sembé are voracious and
for quicker results a close relative must be sacrificed – father,
mother, sister, but preferably the person's own child.

It was George Moutaka who told you Augustin Biampandou was one of the most faithful followers of the
magical-religious sects of that region, and that he already
donated a substantial part of his fortune to them. It only
became known after Samantha's death that the girl's mother
was one of the most famous prostitutes of the Trois-Cents, one
Moleka Loketo. The Pontenegrins claimed she was the most
beautiful woman ever to have come from the other Congo
where, at the age of seventeen, she pursued the profession
of streetwalker, servicing a circle of powerful men, some of
whom hired her services for their trips abroad. At receptions
she played the role of politician's wife or official companion.
In addition, all these politicians were convinced that having
her in their bed would increase their power, and swore that
if you slept with a woman who has intimate relations with
powerful men you would be gifted with their powers and
then gain dominance over them, or even wipe them out and
take their place.

Augustin Biampandou used to send his chauffeur to the
Trois-Cents, and the Mercedes would return an hour later
with Moleka Loketo inside it. The relationship lasted over a
year, till one day the streetwalker informed Augustin Biampandou that she was pregnant. Immediately she became
persona non grata at his residence. Moleka Loketo gave birth at
Adolphe-Cissé hospital, and received not a single visit from
Augustin Biampandou. The day she left hospital she prepared
a little basket, wrapped the baby inside it, and took a taxi
to the centre of town. She rang at the door of her daughter's father's residence, put down the basket, and got back
into the taxi waiting for her a few blocks up. The baby's cries
were so piercing, the neighbours became curious. A security

guard emerged from the residence and took charge of the baby, while, from the vantage point of his balcony, Augustin Biampandou looked upon the basket and the baby, whose voice was now half worn out from crying. He would call her Samantha, after his deceased younger sister, whom the people of Pointe Noire were certain he had sacrificed in order to further solidify his links with president Papa Mokonzi Ayé alias Zarathustra. So Samantha grew up with no parental figure in her life apart from this father who had never married and who provided for her education. There was also the presence of Angelou, who no one in the town believed performed merely the role of house sorcerer.

Samantha was still a pupil at the French lycée when she disappeared. She had her own chauffeur to drive her everywhere, to piano lessons, violin lessons, tennis and swimming. In the town she was known by everyone as 'Daddy's little girl'.

You placed the main courses on the table in front of Augustin Biampandou and the three teenage girls. You stood a little way off behind him, but facing the three girls, with a view of the whole dining room. The Director of the Seaport kept turning round; he had his eye on you, as though preoccupied by your presence. Occasionally, thinking you might have made a mistake, you'd go back over to the table; the man was leaning towards the three girls, talking, then would break off. This game continued through to dessert, and even when the four of them got up to make for the exit and go over to the Atlantic Palace, the direct competitor of the Victory Palace, but definitely the hotel favoured by members of the government.

As he was leaving the building you said to yourself this really was a very powerful man, and George Moutaka was not wrong when he announced, with his finger pointing towards the sky, that Augustin Biampandou was quite some-body. 'The right hand of God' and President of the Republic had met more than forty years before when Papa Mokonzi Ayé alias Zarathustra, having completed his military train-ing at Saint-Cyr in France, was appointed Head of General Military Staff in Pointe-Noire, where Augustin Biampandou was working at the Supply Corps and would shortly join the Mayor of Pointe-Noire's team. It was he who introduced the president to Antoinette-Joséphine Koudia, the future First Lady. She worked as a secretary at the Mairie in Pointe-Noire where Augustin Biampandou had become deputy mayor in charge of finance. The future president regularly invited him to his house and was eternally grateful to him for having introduced him to the love of his life. When a rumour ran round that a coup d'état was being planned in Brazzaville with the support of the French, who were no longer in the good books of the ruling regime, the Saint-Cyr graduate was urgently summoned by President Bernard Molelas to be in charge of the hunting-down of insurgents staked out with their heavy artillery in the Bacongo region, which was known for its hostility to the government. What happened next was later referred to in the country as a 'coup d'état within an ongoing coup d'état'. Papa Mokonzi Ayé alias Zarathustra worked behind the scenes with the French, who promised he would be given recognition if he succeeded in overthrow-ing the current regime. Since he already had the respect of the National Popular Army thanks to his Saint-Cyr prestige, he took control of operations and within two hours Bernard Molelas had ceased to be President of the Republic, though it was he who had mostly opened the gates of the presiden-tial palace to Papa Mokonzi Ayé, in the belief that the latter was acting in the interests of the country. He allowed the deposed president to cross the river to the other Congo and from there fly to Brussels, then London, as he wanted nothing more to do with France and would remain in exile in Great

Britain for a further fifteen years before his death from pancreatic cancer.

Augustin Biampandou could have agreed to join the government. After all, the woman he had introduced to the president had become First Lady, and she would have spoken to her husband on his behalf. But he was more interested in making money, and he couldn't do that from inside a ministry. The president lined his pockets as he pleased, granted him favours, sent him on missions from which he returned with 'sacks-full of dollars', as the Pontenegrins said. He lived like this, changing luxury cars every three months, travelling in the president's private jets, playing golf with presidential families in neighbouring countries who invited him into their palaces and would not let him leave without giving him 'a little something'. In his view this was the best way to live one's life, always paying cash, avoiding tax, using backhanders to get what you wanted. The Pointe-Noire police were at his beck and call, magistrates came to dine at his residence, the president himself secretly ran into several of his feticheurs at Augustin Biampandou's house. His aim was to achieve a life lived in the utmost opulence and to this end he dreamed of directing one of the most coveted structures in the whole country, the Pointe-Noire Seaport. The Head of State, who at first had been categorically opposed to this, since it meant ousting his own son, made a spectacular U-turn when Augustin Biampandou returned from his homeland in the north and renewed his request. He reminded the president that he had been one of his advisors in the famous affair of Frère-Lachaise and the Cemetery of the Rich, which had been the talk of the town and almost thrown the country into civil war. It was he, the Right Hand of God, who had calmed down the most rebellious rich folk and got them to continue to support Papa Mokonzi Ayé alias Zarathustra. And the wealthy owed the successful acquisition of a cemetery of their own not far from the Côte Sauvage to his bribing the landowners to give up their land for the project. He also promised them that what they bought in Europe would never be taxed at the port of Pointe-Noire, be it heavy lorries, buses or luxury cars. Without such compensation the seizing of land from certain Pontenegrins who had inherited it from their ancestors of the Vili ethnicity would have plunged the city into a confrontation which the government would have found it hard to dig its way out of.

Broadly speaking, though power came from the political capital, Augustin Biampandou was the eye of the President of the Republic in the town economy, one of whose lungs was the seaport. He secured electoral support for the president in Pointe-Noire, where the 'Right Hand of God' ensured by all possible means, usually intimidation, but above all his affiliation with occult forces, that his life-long friend would never be deposed.

Papa Mokonzi Ayé alias Zarathustra had signed the order appointing Augustin Biampandou Director General of the Pointe-Noire Seaport and bringing an end to the mandate of his own son, who, the next day, took up the post of Director General of the Congo–Ocean Railway, his predecessor being demoted to the rank of Deputy Director...

The Woman in White

———

SINCE YOU LEFT FRÈRE-LACHAISE and started walking down the rue du Repos, you feel like everything around you is in motion, that the sound of your footsteps on the asphalt have become so mechanical you've ceased to hear them. You don't even know now how far you've walked, your mind is so focussed on your final hours on this earth.

Your huge shoes feel light, and with this regained fleetness of foot you can move forward without fatigue or difficulty. Not a single motorist has passed in either direction, and it's not far now to the centre of town.

You don't know how you should hold your spear and since you're likely to meet people, insomniacs, or late-night partiers leaving bars, you decide to undo your trousers, holding the weapon behind your back, under your jacket, then tightening your belt to hold it in place.

Now the spear is wedged there, you can feel the handle rubbing above your butt, but your hands are free and you can walk along unencumbered. There's only half an hour to go. Your gaze is fixed on the horizon while images from the final hours of your life continue to float before your eyes...

That afternoon, the day after 15 August, you found yourself, against your will, trapped inside Augustin Biampandou's house. He himself was on his way down the steps to your level while the guard had positioned himself by the exit, ensuring you remained imprisoned in the residence, unable to leave it except with the agreement of the Director of the Pointe-Noire Seaport. What intrigued you was the sense that you'd been expected, not by Adeline, whom you still hadn't seen, but by a small welcome committee comprising the influential man himself and his guard dog. The flowers you had brought for Adeline were lying on the ground and seemed suddenly to have withered.

There followed a long silence, during which the guard and Augustin Biampandou looked at each other as though waiting to give a signal, then their eyes turned on you, till the Director of the Seaport gave a nod to his subaltern, who finally pointed to the little sitting area that had been set up on the opposite side of the yard, beneath a thatch, with an oval table and wicker chairs, the biggest of which, angled towards the entrance, was for Augustin Biampandou himself.

Angelou had gone out, dressed in white wraps. Like most Pontenegrins you knew that this was the costume worn by healing women, particularly of the northern sorcerers from the region of the 'Right Hand of God'. You also knew that most rich and influential people lived with a woman who was either a healer or a house sorcerer, or both. The same person also carried out the duties of a maid, but it was not uncommon for her to be the mistress of the important person. Healers and sorcerers thus lived under the rich man's roof till the end of their own life or that of the individual protecting them. It was hard to dismiss them because the contract was presumed to have been signed in the presence of the spirits of the ancestors and any breach would incur their wrath. The sorcerer was also there to support and advise the man under their protection in any life-changing decisions he might have to take. She must pick up in advance on anything bad that might happen to the house or its master, for she was said to have four eyes, counting the ones in the back of her head that only initiates could see.

You were not wrong: Angelou was indeed both sorcerer and a servant – the very one who had taken Samantha under her wing from the first day she had been left outside the front door of the residence by her biological mother, Moleka Loketo. Back then, in her role of advisor, Angelou had told Augustin that this was no trivial gesture, that it was modelled on a famous episode in the Bible, and that, without wishing to overstate things, the abandoning of the little girl outside the front door reminded her of the child who had been placed in a basket of papyrus and left among the reeds at the edge of the Nile. And this child was then found by the daughter of the King of Egypt on her way to the river to bathe. The baby she drew from the waters would become Moses, 'the one drawn from the waters', just like Samantha, who might also be said to have been 'drawn from the ocean'.

Augustin Biampandou had resolved to rid himself of the little girl and send her to an orphanage in Loango.

Angelou intervened:

'Children who are abandoned like that will always feel they have a mission to accomplish, and you don't know what your daughter's might be... She must stay with us. I will look after her as if I'd given birth to her myself!'

She warned him not to harm a single hair on the girl's head.

'If you don't change your behaviour, Samantha may be the source of your downfall...'

But the Director of the Seaport did not heed the advice of the woman in white. He took as much as suited him, and when he wanted to dispense with her services, he went directly up north to consult different sorcerers, considering his own to be too moderate and compassionate to protect him.

So he swept aside her entreaties when she revealed to him, a week before 15 August, that she had started to see the defunct Samantha wandering ever closer to the residence, as though she had decided it was time to confront her father. She added that at night Samantha came in by scaling the wall behind the property or through the main entrance, blowing into the nostrils of the guard to put him into a deep sleep that lasted hours, before she sat down under the thatch, in her father's wicker chair, only leaving at dawn.

Angelou, who lived on the ground floor, would stand on tiptoe and see Samantha circling the yard while the guard snored with his weapon a good metre out of reach. It was clear to the erstwhile nanny – and proxy mother – that Samantha was in no way still the little girl who used to snuggle into her arms. She had become a young woman, with her hair pulled back off her face. Sometimes, if she looked too closely, the woman in white could see Samantha transform into her constituent body parts, some of which looked as though they had been eaten by fish. The girl would then enact her ordeal with the two determined, hooded men, who had first smothered her, then divided up her organs for the sacrifice demanded of the Director of the Seaport by the sorcerers from up north. Angelou understood that Samantha's blood contained the power of the dead from her father's region, who wandered round in human guise, assuming at will the features of whoever they chose.

In this case, whether the girl was called Adeline or Samantha, she was one and the same, and she would use every trick in the book to fulfil her mission. . .

Angelou had also pointed out to her boss that by attending the lunch at the Victory Palace he would be signing his own death warrant. The agent of his dispatch to the world beyond would be in the room, perfectly disguised. It would be someone whose presence he for once would 'feel', though until then the Director of the Seaport would have scarcely noticed them.

Augustin Biampandou could still have countered this premonition by cancelling his lunch at the hotel. Out of the question, he raged. And he became even more jumpy when the cabinet office called from Brazzaville to check he would be looking after the three ministers arriving for the parade on 14 August. He knew what 'looking after' meant and it didn't mean drawing up an official timetable for them, there were other people to do that; besides, these politicians didn't give a damn for the timetable. Their main interest was quite clear, and Augustin Biampandou was well aware, having already organised such programmes for the president and his Prime Minister: they should not feel lonely in their hotel. And the only kind of company they desired was the kind that increased their power, their influence. They demanded 'young chicks', to use their own expression.

Augustin Biampandou sent out his 'minions' into the poorer districts, to source the necessary for these important people, and at one o'clock he sat down to eat with three teenagers, just as you were being summoned to the restaurant to wait on them. Behind you, at the bar, you were quite unaware it was Samantha serving the cocktails, in the guise of Xavière, whose presence might have raised questions, since she had called in that morning to tell the boss that she wasn't feeling well and would be taking the day off. Samantha even managed to recreate to perfection the slight scowl often worn by the waitress. While the Director of the Seaport's daughter prepared glasses of vodka for the girls her father had invited to lunch, the staff assumed it was being done by their colleague, Xavière...

The woman in white had 'seen' all this, and informed Augustin Biampandou as he was getting ready to go over to the Victory Palace:

'The omens are terrible, worse than they've ever been. . . I see an oddly dressed young man dancing with Samantha in a discotheque. . .'

'What, you're saying someone else has seen Samantha? Are you raving mad, Angelou? The child's got such a hold on you, you see nothing but her!'

'I'm not raving, I've never raved. Tell me one time I had a vision that didn't come true!'

The Director of the Seaport said nothing, silently capitulating to this woman who had been recommended to him decades earlier by one of his Sembé aunts, Tala-Tala Ekossiyo, held to be the most powerful sorcerer in the history of the region. Angelou was a descendant of the sorcerer caste of Sembé, in the north. It was said that their family could detect people concealed in human guise so as to stay among the living and meddle in all kinds of business. Her grandmother and mother had been sorcerers too, and when they died they passed on their powers to the next generation. No one left any private property, as they always lived in the houses of the rich, with guaranteed board, lodging and a modest salary. On her side of the family, Angelou was the only person not issued from a sexual relation with the person the sorcerer was protecting. Her grandmother and mother were both born of adultery and had replaced their boss's wife after she died. They didn't marry the wealthy man, but spent the rest of their lives at his side, caring for his children, meeting his every desire, protecting him to the end of his days.

'We can still stop this happening, but you must be merciful to the young man in the strange clothes. . .'

'What does that mean?' the Director of the Seaport snapped, scarcely able to hide his inner rage.

'It means you mustn't let your anger get the better of you. If the young man dies, the prophecy will come to pass, Samantha will tell the spirit of the young man where to find whoever cast her into the angry waters. That means you – and don't try hoodwinking me with some cock-and-bullshit about the tramps on the Côte Sauvage or a swimming accident.'

'The story about Samantha mustn't get back into the news...'

'Too late, boss – all I'm seeing is Samantha's body parts being spewed up by sea creatures. Samantha's immortal remains are wandering about here, and will not rest till you have died. Wherever you are, there too is your daughter...'

'Even now?'

Angelou lowered her gaze. 'I cannot answer that.'

Then Augustin Biampandou simply yelled:

'All right, I'm ready! What will be will be! Let the young man come!'

The Walk

—

SO THERE YOU WERE, inside the residence, face to face with the man you waited on two days before at the Victory Palace, whom you'd found so nervous and restless with his guests.

Angelou came up and asked what you would like to drink. Nothing, you said, but judging by Augustin Biampandou's attitude, this was the wrong answer, so you opted for a Coca-Cola.

The woman in white picked up the bunch of flowers lying on the floor, gave you a look, then followed Augustin Biampandou into the house.

The two of them re-emerged about ten minutes later, the sorcerer carrying a tray of drinks and avoiding your gaze.

Your glass was already full, as was that of Augustin Biampandou, who had ordered a Chivas.

He swallowed a gulp of his whiskey and asked in a firm voice:

'Who sent you here, then? Is this some stunt by the Victory Palace? You looked very jumpy when you were serving me. What are you up to?'

Your throat was tight with fear; you didn't know how to

answer Augustin Biampandou. His eyes were on stalks now. You picked up your glass and drank, to gain time.

The woman in white gave you one last look, then one to the guard, who was still holding his weapon, then went and shut herself up inside the house.

Taking your courage in both hands, you stood up:

'I think I'd better go now, Monsieur Biampandou. . .'

'Sit down, you little fool!' he roared, as the guard stepped close, his weapon just centimetres from your skull. 'Empty your glass and get out now!'

You picked up your glass, took a few mouthfuls, and drank it dry. It tasted of spices and kaolin.

You turned to look at the guard, then back at Augustin Biampandou, who, impassively now, signalled to his guard to show you to the exit. . .

Once you had been pushed out like one of the unclean by the security guard, you walked along the Côte Sauvage, with your hands clasped behind your back. You didn't realise you were talking to yourself. That the waves seemed to answer. To hell with their roar.

You were recalling the evening at the Ceremonial, images passing before your eyes: the 'belly to belly' rumba, the excited couples all around, the copious quantities of rum, the women cheering you on, the salsa dancers, male and female, the close embrace, how you stroked Adeline's temples, or rather Samantha's. The atmosphere was like in a dream; time seemed so short, everything happened so fast, and a strange dizziness had come over you both. You gave up the struggle and let yourself go with the flow.

Deep in your thoughts, swept along by your inner turmoil, haunted by your dance partner's face, you almost fell as you stumbled across a small mound of sand.

At the last minute, you saved yourself.

Realising you must have stepped on something, you glanced down: it was the orange crepe jacket with the broad cuffs you'd lent to Samantha alias Adeline, which now lay hidden in the sand.

This discovery gave you a jolt: you immediately picked up your piece of clothing and ran in the direction of the Place Félix-Éboué, where you jumped into a taxi.

When you got home you quickly paid your fare and without saying goodbye to the driver ran inside the house.

Mâ Lembé wasn't there. You went straight to your room, shivering increasingly with cold; you heard your stomach churning, then your body grew heavier, and you collapsed onto your bed.

Then suddenly darkness fell, and five days later you felt a great jolt and the earth split open beneath you and first the cyclone sucked you up, then spat you out on a little mound with a brand-new wooden cross on top.

Which is how you became a resident of Frère-Lachaise...

Like the Death Throes of a Wild Beast

———

BY NOW YOU'VE ARRIVED at the Place Félix-Éboué.

You walk down the street that has become so familiar, which leads to the Côte Sauvage, the wharf and the Cemetery of the Rich.

You meet not one single vehicle; it must be gone half past two in the morning. You're used to this area now, and nothing surprises you; these sumptuous houses, the walls between the properties painted with quicklime.

You take out your spear, and the blade gleams in the reflection of the half-moon above. You hold it in your right hand and walk slowly, almost breaking your movement down into little parts, eyes to the ground. Never have you felt so determined, nor possessed by such an inexplicable feeling of strength.

You arrive at the residence of Augustin Biampandou, and stop outside the gates.

You hesitate a few minutes, then decide to walk round the property. Suddenly you realise you possess a suppleness which enables you to climb up the wall of the residence and jump down into the familiar courtyard.

The thatched area is all tidy; the chairs have been turned over and arranged around the oval table – which brings back memories of the spicy Coca-Cola tasting of kaolin.

The guard is asleep on a mattress on the ground, up against the gate. You lean down and blow a long breath into his nose. His snoring increases and now can be heard from beyond the precincts of the house.

You climb the flights of steps leading to the landing from which the Director of the Seaport looked down at you a few days ago.

You find yourself in the salon, which is lit by a tiny lamp on a dresser opposite. You are dazzled by the splendour of this luxurious, modern interior, the marble, the golden drapes, the huge living space, the four sofas with huge cushions and, above you, the giant crystal chandelier hanging from the ceiling.

To your right is a corridor, to your left a staircase.

You head for the corridor, which leads to a small apartment. You push the half-open door.

You hold up your spear and enter.

A pair of women's shoes are lying in the middle of the main room. The bedroom is opposite, and this door, too, stands halfway open. You open it wide and find yourself looking at a woman you know, Angelou.

She is stretched out by the bath tub, lifeless, her eyes rolled upwards, mouth smeared with an ochre powder.

You pick up the piece of paper lying close by and read the words: 'I told you he would return. Adieu.'

You go back into the main room and make for the staircase, using your spear as support.

You reach the first floor.

The view is of the Côte Sauvage, you can see the wharf from here. By night it looks like a decapitated giraffe searching for its head in the ocean.

A little further off are the dazzling lights of the Cemetery of the Rich.

Your intuition tells you that of the five doors ranged in a semi-circle, the middle one leads to Augustin Biampandou's room.

You are not wrong.

Like the others, it is open, and you slip in.

From his extremely spacious room, Augustin Biampandou has a view of the Seaport.

He is snoring; you can make out the shape of his huge body under the heavy covers. You go towards the bed, walk round one side and, throwing one last glance at the Pointe-Noire Seaport, you grasp the shaft of your spear in both hands, swing it back, raising both hands above your head, grit your teeth, close your eyes for a few seconds, then plunge the weapon into the solid form. Without looking at the red stain seeping out onto the white covers, you head off towards the stairs.

From down on the ground floor you can hear groaning, like a wild creature in its death throes, the man who up to this moment had been one of the most powerful forces in the city. . .

The Farewell

———

YOU'RE WALKING ON THE CÔTE SAUVAGE, by the same path as when you found your jacket buried in the sand.

You're shaking all over, but also have a feeling of satisfaction and relief. Soon the entire city of Pointe-Noire will learn of Augustin Biampandou's death, and all sorts of theories will be produced to explain it.

The sea is calm, it's rare to find it looking so serene. A light wind brushes against your ears. You know if you turn round now you will see Samantha.

Yes, there she is, this wind at your ears is her breath, her very presence.

You walk towards the Joli-Soir district and she follows.

She's not sure exactly where you're going now, but she's behind you like your shadow. . .

At last you arrive at the dance bar, Joli-Soir. It's closed now, the owner's mark of respect in your memory. He'll open again tomorrow, once the public has left Mâ Lembé's house, and doesn't know yet that he'll have to shut up shop again at the announcement of Augustin Biampandou's passing. And this time not just a single sector but the entire town will be plunged into mourning, and President Papa Mokonzi Ayé alias Zarathustra himself will come to the funeral, which will be nothing like your own.

There are still a few people at your place, but not as many as during the four days of your wake, just Sabine Bouanga and the other women from the Grand Marché. They will stay to support your grandmother over the coming weeks. She will not sleep alone in this house in the days to come, she'll stay with each of her colleagues in turn; they'll try to assuage her grief, to talk with her, lest your absence drag her away into the other world before her time.

You're outside the entrance to the plot now.
You'd like to see Mâ Lembé one last time, to say goodbye. Your eyes seek her out among the other tradeswomen sitting outside in a circle, eating. There's no electricity at your house, so they've lit candles to boost the light from the two storm lamps in the middle of the circle. Sabine Bouanga seems to be giving instructions and even here she stands out as someone who doesn't just rule the roost at the Grand Marché, but who is by nature charismatic and reassuring, and you are glad that she is there with Mâ Lembé.

An old lady with a stick, dressed in white, comes out from the house and joins the group of women. Her head is covered with a black scarf. You can only see her profile, but you know it is Mâ Lembé.

You wish she would look across to this side of the rue du Joli-Soir. Alas, as during the longest dream of your death when you saw her busy with your funeral, she once more has her back to you and is facing Sabine Bouanga, while she's the one looking your way.

You won't budge from this spot till you have seen your grandmother's face; she has to know that you have been here.

A dog barks behind you. It's your last chance, you tell yourself. It's a black dog. You go towards him. His desperate bark arouses the curiosity of the tradeswomen, and they all turn round and point out the presence of the animal to Mâ Lembé.

'Over there, by the entrance to the yard!' cries Sabine Bouanga.

Mâ Lembé turns and your eyes meet hers. Something happens that you can't explain. A sense of peace, like the feeling you had when you'd finished off Augustin Biampandou. Complete happiness, at which you blink for a moment, and fill your ribcage with breath.

You look again, and again see your grandmother's eyes, damp and filled with concern. By the light of the candles you see her glistening tears, infectious tears, and you start to weep too, but your tears only flow on the inside.

The dog has vanished. Mâ Lembé gets up to come to the entrance to the plot and, walking towards you, says:

'Is that you, Liwa?'

You would like to speak but no words come. So you take a step back, then another one, and you run from this place, while your grandmother's voice goes on calling with a dying fall...

You pay no attention to Samantha, who is still behind you. She has watched from a distance as you approached Mâ Lembé. She has seen that this is a family unlike one from the centre of town.

You reach the rue du Repos and without turning round you say:

'Go back to the Cemetery of the Rich now, Samantha, we part company here. . .'

'But I want to live with you.'

'Your place is with them, not here at Frère-Lachaise. . .'

'I won't rest in peace at the Cemetery of the Rich and they'll bury my father there soon.'

As you make your way up the rue du Repos with Samantha by your side, you for once give a little smile, and hear in your head the echo of the Crow Woman's words:

'The noblest thing you could do would be to return to the land of the living and perform an act establishing your greatness for all eternity, breathing life and love into those from whom it has unjustly been withheld. . .'

Translator's Note

———

ALAIN MABANCKOU ONCE SPOKE of himself as a migratory bird, 'who remembers the country he's come from but chooses to stay and sing on the branch where he's perched.' Although it is an inspired metaphor for his childhood in Congo-Brazzaville, his student and early professional years in France, his life today as an academic on the west coast of the United States, it is almost too easy a characterisation. Come springtime, migratory birds head home, but Alain does not – cannot – for the moment, return to the country of his birth. He lives today between California and Paris. It is a life spent living and writing, though, never waiting. The triangle on the map is fully completed through his writing.

Alain's mother, Pauline, gave birth to him a few years after the end of French colonial rule, in 1966, two years before power was seized by President Marien Ngouabi. Alain was eleven when the assassination of Ngouabi threw the country into turmoil. The long, self-serving rule of Sassou Nguesso and his family, with a five-year interruption at the fall of the Soviet Union, continues today, its roots in the complex soil of Congo-Brazzaville, its leaves in the boardrooms of oil companies, its flowering in the chic designer boutiques of the boulevard Saint-Germain. Alain is just as critical – more so, possibly – of the present-day regime in Congo-Brazzaville as he is of French colonial rule. The delicious sound of eggshells crunching underfoot is one of the hallmarks of his work.

The world of Alain's childhood was a mish-mash of busy African city, feral dogs, the wild shore of the Congo river where it meets the Atlantic, skies across which the first planes to Europe and the States drew their chalky arrows, aromatic street food, gossip and mangled political rumour; a hash of colonial and multi-tribal history. From this mix Alain creates his own, unique dish, stirred and brewed in a *marmite* – a melting pot – of ingredients: memory, lyricism, slapstick, political critique, African tribal lore and allusions to the great, beloved literature of France – learned at the school desk in the Karl Marx College in Pointe-Noire and from books discarded by French visitors at his stepfather's place of work, the Victory Palace hotel.

Alain's writing is complex. That doesn't mean it is complex, always, to translate it from French into English. After all, a translator's task is not to explain a text, it is to offer it to readers in their own language, without trappings or embellishment.

The challenges of translation are almost never to do with figuring out what the word for this or that is. A pianist will not pause to wonder where a note is on the keyboard, or to identify that black dot three spaces above middle C. The real questions are – what is that song? Where is that phrase going? How does it echo, without replicating, the one so like it three pages earlier, or the phrase in a poem in the author's head that he scarcely knew was there? *Dealing with the Dead* is the first work by Alain (and we are on our seventh together) for which I have had an audio reading by him playing through my headphones. To hear the familiar cadences and emphases as his genial, trenchant, ironic voice speaks the text – expressing his own personality as I understand it, knowing him a little, knowing his work so well – is extraordinary, like hearing a composer perform their own work. 'We have a bizarre accent,' a character says in *Black Bazaar*. 'You can hear it when we write.' Not all sentences are made to be spoken out loud, not all utterances are made to be written down, but in Alain's work there is a beautiful counterpoint of the oral and the literary, reflecting the inner soundscape of this deeply literary, street-happy man with the rusty, resonant voice. I say street-happy – you only have to look at his Instagram posts, the images of him dressed in the vibrant colours of the Sapeur, sauntering by the ocean in LA, or down a Parisian passageway, to know this is a man who stops and talks, shares a joke, listens, and moves on. Perhaps he is on his way to lecture at the Collège de France, or to his students at UCLA, or heading for a dance club. The visual image of him, and the sound of his voice – these are important to the translator too. They must be present in the strings of words you find to represent his own.

Alain writes in French. His French style is fusion, not in its methods but its ingredients. His French is the French of the Académie Française: limpid, elegant, polished as crystal on a dining table, though it might be filled with finest claret or roughest palm wine. French is his writing language. It was his passport to France in 1988, aged twenty-two. His English is pretty perfect. It must have a US accent by now. But his writing roots are European, and he sticks with them, which is why in part he has a British translator.

Dealing with the Dead is the story of Liwa, who wakes one day in the cemetery where, three days earlier, he was buried, at the age of twenty-four. His death at the hands of politically motivated men occurs, and is mourned, in a context of tribal customs and beliefs, so the prose comes seasoned with terms from one of the many African languages Alain speaks and features spears and Kalashnikovs, plant poisons, resurrections, *féticheurs* (witch doctors? fetishers? fetishists? – those eggshells again), zombies, pork and plantain, huts and fancy houses in the chic business quarters of the city. Each of the characters who appears to Liwa in the cemetery delivers an account of their misadventures. The rhythms are constantly changing, becoming more urgent, fading away into lyrical recollection, speeding up in anger, rarely, if ever, falling silent. There is always a bird on a branch above, listening, or a character lurking in the background, pretending not to hear.

There are particular 'problems' – translating hallowed lines from a poem by Tati-Loutard, rendering an absurd political speech recited 'from memory' by someone who heard it twenty years ago, or grappling with puns: an error that mangles the sense of a gravestone epitaph has to work as well in English as it does in French. Or splitting open the joke when he calls the expensive residential quarter in Pointe-Noire the *quartier* MTV, or 'M'as Tu Vu?' – alluding both to the availability of Euro satellite TV in these houses and to the French expression for Showing Off. Almost without thinking, it seems, Alain plays avant-garde semiotic games that occupy many pages of analysis in critical appraisals of his work. As a translator you have to be aware of them.

Have to? Maybe not. It's not vital the translator recognise in Liwa's relationship with his grandmother an echo of Proust's narrator with his grandmother at Balbec. Or that 'The longest dream of my death' echoes the title of 'The Longest Dream of History', volume 4 of which, about Lyautey, a French white colonial 'Empire Builder', is called 'The African; or the Massacred Dream'. Or that the second-person singular narrative form used throughout – 'you wake', etc. – is identical to that used by Nathaniel Hawthorne in his 1835 short story about waking from death, 'The Haunted Mind'.

But to be curious about these things puts you beside the author on that branch, listening, feeling the same breezes, sensitive to the same swaying movements of the tree, the same shifts of current in the air. The writer himself, as Proust pointed out, already understands and practises the translator's art: 'I realised that the essential book, the one true book, is one that the great writer does not need to invent, since it already exists in every one of us – they need only translate it.'

Helen Stevenson